Christmas Crazy

By

Kathi Daley

Chapter 1

Every year between the dates of December 1 and December 24, a strange and wonderful insanity hits my hometown of Ashton Falls. Most refer to this phenomenon as Christmas Spirit, but I've been around long enough to know that *spirit* usually translates to *insanity*, which brings on a phenomenon I like to refer to as Christmas Crazy.

For those of you I haven't yet met, my name is Zoe Donovan. I am a third-generation Ashtonite (our unofficial name for the citizens of our little community). I often complain about the long hours required to pull off the biggest and best Christmas extravaganza this side of, well, anywhere, but truth be told, I love everything about this hectic but wonderful time of year.

My story began on a snowy Tuesday in early December. The agglomeration of Christmas hysteria was just beginning and most were still happily unaware of the frenzy that would soon engulf our little town. Charlie, my half Tibetan terrier/half mystery dog, and I had just left the high school, where we met with Principal Joe Lamé—pronounced La-mae with an exaggerated accent—and were on our way to the regular Tuesday morning breakfast meeting of the Ashton Falls Events Committee. Although it was only December 3, the entire town was decked out in holiday splendor reminiscent of an old-fashioned Christmas village.

I tried to let the magic of the season calm my restless thoughts as I drove through the festively decorated village, but the uncertainty of the request I planned to make at the committee meeting weighed heavily on my mind. I slowed my truck slightly as a group of seniors from the center crossed the street in front of the Rotary tree lot on their way to the town square. Every year Gabe Turner, the owner of a local lumber company, volunteers his services to cut the most inimitable tree he can find, and every year dozens of residents descend on the town square to string lights and hang ornaments, creating an extravagant hallmark worthy of a Lifetime original movie.

I waved at Hazel Hampton as she struggled with one of the giant wreaths being installed on every lamppost along Main Street. The lampposts had been donated by my mother's family for the town's fiftieth anniversary celebration. At first I thought the lights— white wrought iron with fancy lantern-shaped lights, three to a post—a bit ostentatious for our rugged little town, but as time has passed, the beacons have grown on me.

"Do you need any help?" I asked as I pulled my truck over to the side of the road.

"Actually, I could use a hand," Hazel, our town librarian, replied. "Go ahead and park that monster of yours, then come back around. I'll wait for you."

I agreed to Hazel's suggestion and pulled around to enter the parking area behind Rosie's Cafe. I looked for a spot at the back of the lot, where I'd have plenty of room to maneuver. After I'd parked carefully, Charlie and I headed back around to the street to help Hazel as promised. As I looked up and down Main Street, I noticed that the decorating crew had managed to transform our little hamlet in just a few short hours. In addition to the giant evergreen wreaths with bright red bows that hung on every lamppost, volunteers from the fire department were stringing colored lights across the street at every intersection. Christmas carols blasted from storefronts along the main drag as local shop owners decorated their windows with tiny villages that told a story if you viewed the displays in order from west to east.

"It's beginning to look a lot like Christmas." I tried for a light tone as Charlie and I joined Hazel.

"I just love this time of year." Hazel smiled. "And it's so nice that Mother Nature provided us with snow for our decorating party. It really adds to the ambience."

I looked at the flakes that danced and swayed as they floated gently to the ground. It had been snowing steadily since before Thanksgiving, but there's something about Christmas snow that creates a cozy feeling that just cannot be duplicated by ordinary winter snow. Hazel held the ladder while I climbed up and attempted to hang the wreath.

Hazel is a feisty sixty-two-year-old with tidy brown hair, sharp chiseled features, and a tall, lanky frame who has never married or had children of her own but is wildly popular with the under-ten population of our little town. In addition to running the library, she serves on the community events committee, volunteers for the local children's theater, and participates in the book club, which Charlie and I attend on Thursday nights.

"Are you coming in for the meeting?" I wondered. Every Tuesday morning the Ashton Falls Events Committee has a breakfast in the back room of Rosie's Cafe, where we cook up plans for the myriad of celebrations we organize as part of our attempts to balance the town's budget.

"Yeah. I just have two more wreaths and then I should be done. If you can lend a hand, it should only take a few minutes."

I climbed to the top rung of the ladder and still couldn't reach the destination intended for the wreath. Not one to give up, I stood on my tiptoes, reached as far as my arm would extend, and finally looped the wreath on one of the permanently installed hooks that worked equally well for Halloween pumpkins, spring flowers, or Fourth of July flags.

I climbed down the ladder and we moved on to the next lamppost. "Who was helping you before I came along?" Perhaps this particular job was better suited for someone with a bit more height.

"Your dad, but he got called over to help with the light-stringing committee."

My dad, Hank Donovan, is a volunteer firefighter and local business owner. Like Hazel and me, he is a member of the planning committee. "Did he say whether he planned to come to the meeting?"

"I believe he does," Hazel confirmed as we finished wreath number two—thank God someone had installed this hook a bit lower and I was able to hang the dang thing without risking my life—and moved on to wreath number three. Too bad my sort-of boyfriend, Zak, wasn't around. At well over six foot tall, he'd have the wreaths hung in no time.

"I can't believe how fantastic the town looks," I said, admiring the wonderland that had been created along the main corridor from my vantage point high atop the ladder as I struggled to hang the wreath Hazel had handed me. "I feel like I live in a real live Santa's village. Now all we need are a few elves and a herd of reindeer."

"I imagine both will be making an appearance at some point during the month."

"Any more wreaths?" I asked.

"No, I think that's it. Let's head inside," Hazel suggested as she folded up the ladder. "I could really go for a nice hot cup of coffee and one of Rosie's homemade pastries. I'm sure she has something special for the meeting."

The thought of pastries made my mouth water, even though Charlie and I had already consumed a hearty breakfast at the boathouse we call home. I glanced at my dad as he waved at me from across the street. While many of the people I know look nothing like their parents, I've always felt that I was a unique combination of mine. In addition to my dad's stick-thin physique, I also inherited his speckling of freckles, round face, and thick curly hair, a deep chestnut brown that most days is a wild mess that I just braid or pull back with a large clip. I've been told I have my mother's eyes, sort of an intense yet unusual piercing blue with long, thick lashes, as well as her wide, full-lipped smile. Most days I am satisfied with the image looking back at me in the mirror, although I have to admit there are times I wish for a statuesque frame and straight, easy-to-manage hair.

After stashing the ladder, Hazel and I headed into Rosie's, a quintessential small-town cafe. On any given day, during the hours between six a.m. and two p.m., locals and visitors alike gather to share a meal and catch up on the latest news. In deference to the holiday season, Rosie had decorated her window with a holiday scene, one of the many to be found along Main Street. Each scene tells part of a story, and Rosie's part is a depiction of children in a schoolyard, playing on swings, slides, and other playground equipment. In the background there's a forest scene, complete with local animals such as black bears, mule deer, coyotes, and raccoons. I knew that the story for this year was about a raccoon that followed a group of children onto the school bus and ended up in the middle of the city during Christmas. Rosie's is located on the west end of town, near the beginning of the windows. If viewed from west to east, the window displays eventually changed from alpine themes to scenes of holiday shoppers in wonderfully decorated downtown settings. I think my favorite display this year is the one with the large ice-skating rink, made to resemble the one in New York City's Rockefeller Center.

In addition to the window display, a tall but narrow tree near the cash register welcomed guests with colorful ornaments, and real fir wreathes fashioned from tree branches and pinecones were hung on the pine-paneled walls that made up the main dining area.

I'll Be Home for Christmas played softly over the stereo system as I paused to consider the ruckus that was taking place at a table in the back of the room. Someone, who I later determined was none other than Earl Fielder, the town's beloved Santa Claus, was causing a scene because he'd ordered his eggs over easy and apparently they'd arrived over medium. I frowned as the waitress stepped aside and Earl's bearded face appeared. He's about as nice a guy as you'd ever want to meet, so it seemed totally out of character for him to be carrying on in such a public fashion. I considered approaching the table in order to run interference for the waitress, who was both young and new, but Gabe Turner arrived just as I was turning to approach and slid into the booth across from him. Deciding that Gabe had things under control, I continued on to the back of the restaurant.

I settled Charlie in the corner of the conference room where the meeting would be held. Due to health regulations, dogs normally aren't allowed inside the dining area, but Charlie is well-known as a therapy dog, so he's always been given a pass. I brushed the snow from my shoulder before hanging my red ski jacket on a hook in the corner of the room. I briefly admired the Christmas dish display Rosie had arranged on her grandmother's antique hutch before sitting down next to my best friend, Levi Denton, who was talking to my other best friend, Ellie Davis.

Perhaps I should take a moment to catch you up, in case you've missed prior installments of what I've come to refer to as the Levi and Ellie quandary. Levi, Ellie, and I have been best friends since kindergarten, when everyone sat at round tables of three, alphabetically by last name. The three of us had bonded over clay figures and finger paints and have been friends ever since. During our years together, we have enjoyed a comfortable equilibrium as a coterie based on a best friend triad. If you ask me, this dynamic has served us well. The dilemma in our relationship first arose a couple of months ago, when I noticed that Ellie's feelings toward Levi had evolved into something that included romantic undertones. The modification in the previously established group dynamic has created an underlying tension that none of us quite knows how to deal with.

"You made it." Levi kissed me on the cheek.

"I was helping Hazel with the wreaths," I explained.

"You look very Christmassy in your bright red sweater and jingle-bell earrings," Levi admired.

"Thanks. I feel Christmassy." I smiled at Levi, who always has a way of making me feel special. Prior to our current friendship dilemma, there had been a small part of me that wondered if perhaps Levi and *I* would eventually hook up. Not that I spent a lot of time dwelling on the possibility, but he's sweet and considerate and, according to many, a total babe.

"Willa's getting antsy to start." Ellie leaned around Levi so that I could see her. "It seems like everyone is trickling in later than usual."

"Decorating party," I reminded her as I helped myself to one of Rosie's Double Chocolate Apricot Cranberry Bars.

Willa Walton sat down across the table from us. She works for the town of Ashton Falls and acts as a mediator between the committee and the town council. I watched her nervously as she settled her pile of paperwork and smiled at me. I knew that if my crazy plan was going to work, I was going to need her support.

"I'm glad you made it," Willa said. "We've missed you the past couple of weeks."

"I know. I'm sorry I've been missing meetings, but I'm back now," I assured her.

"I'm glad to hear it. We still have a few missing members. Do you know if Zak is going to show?"

"Zak is on the East Coast for a business meeting," I informed Willa. "He won't be back in town until later this week."

Zak Zimmerman is a computer genius, multimillionaire, my new neighbor, and, as I mentioned, my sort-of boyfriend. Zak and I have had a complicated relationship dating back to the seventh grade. During recent months, I've reconciled my old resentment for the man and replaced it with feelings I find as terrifying as they are wonderful.

"Okay, then, let's get started," Willa announced. "Has everyone had a chance to read the minutes of the last meeting?"

The group as a whole nodded their assent as Willa called for a motion to approve.

"As you all know," Willa continued, "the next few weeks are going to be very busy. It's important that we all attend these meetings and stay on top of our assignments. Zoe, are you ready to give your report?"

I quickly gathered my notes. This year I was elected chairperson—against my will, I might add—of the Hometown Christmas celebration, a four-day event that's held every year the weekend before

Christmas. Hometown Christmas began as a fund-raising endeavor, but it has grown into a well-loved event. The shopkeepers along Main Street, as well as many other local citizens, dress up in old-fashioned attire and food and craft vendors, also in costume, are located at various venues around town. Transportation between events is provided by horse-drawn carriages because Main Street is closed to all vehicular traffic.

"Things are going well," I began. "I plan to use the community center as the cornerstone of the event. We'll set up many of the out-of-town vendors as well as the kiddie carnival inside. Not only is the venue located conveniently at the edge of town, but I found out that it will already be decorated; Santa's Village opens the week prior to Hometown Christmas, which will save me hours of garlanding angst."

"Will the food vendors be located in the center as well?" Hazel asked.

"Many of them," I confirmed. "I plan to set up tables near the stage. We have several groups coming in to provide carols to entertain the diners. There will also be music and food vendors set up in a tent in the park."

"What about the strolling carolers?" Willa asked. "They're my favorite part of the event."

"Weather permitting," I confirmed. "We also plan to have a few street vendors selling hot drinks and snacks along the beach walk, as well as sleigh rides through town, a sledding hill behind the high school, and ice skating at Beaver Cove."

"Do you think we should put so many of the vendors indoors?" Hazel asked. "It might take away from the festive feel along Main Street."

"The main reason I decided to move the majority of the vendors inside this year is because of the iffy weather we've had in the past," I explained. "That blizzard we had three years ago almost caused the whole event to be canceled."

"It sounds like you have everything under control," Willa complimented me.

"I do have one request," I said nervously. "And it's kind of a big one, so I really need all of you to consider my proposal before commenting."

"What is it?" Willa asked.

Pretty much everyone at the table was looking at me in both fascination and confusion. I'd thought about pulling Levi, Ellie, and my dad aside and filling them in before the meeting, but the opportunity hadn't presented itself.

"I spoke to Erica Connors from the animal shelter in Bryton Lake this morning. It seems that in the weeks since our local shelter was closed, the number of animals scheduled for termination at the main shelter has increased dramatically. Erica has at least twenty dogs and cats slated for *processing* if they aren't adopted before Christmas."

"What happened?" Hazel asked. "Why the huge increase?"

"Jeremy and I were extremely successful in finding placements for our animals," I said, referring to my former assistant, Jeremy Fisher. "We assisted the other shelters in the county in finding homes for their short-timers as well. I guess the number of adoptions in the county has decreased dramatically since we've been closed, and the number of animals placed in the shelter in Bryton Lake has tripled."

"That's because the animal-patrol guys from the valley are picking up dogs from the lake that never would have been picked up before," Hazel said.

"I've heard that," I agreed.

"So what can we do to help?" Willa asked.

"I'd like to use the high-school gym to hold a pet adoption during Hometown Christmas."

"Won't we need the gym for the Hometown Christmas events?"

"No. I've arranged it so that the gym is totally free."

"Why don't you just have the adoption at the Zoo?" Levi asked.

After the county closed the local animal shelter, Zak had bought the building and renamed it Zoe's Zoo.

"The county won't let us use the building to house animals for even a day until we're fully permitted. I was hoping we'd be up and running in time for the adoption, but it isn't looking good."

"Wouldn't use of the gym be up to the high school?" Hazel asked.

"I checked with them. The gym is reserved for use by the committee for the Christmas event. Initially, I thought about having the food court there, so I applied for the permit on behalf of the committee." I took a deep breath. "I know this is a little out of the box. Not only will I need everyone's support, but I'll need everyone's help as well. Hometown Christmas begins on the nineteenth. I plan to make the trip to Bryton Lake to pick up whatever animals remain on death row that morning. Assuming we don't get all the animals adopted that first day, I'll need community members willing to house unadopted animals until the next day."

"I'll help," Levi assured me.

"Yeah, me, too," Ellie joined in. "In fact, I can borrow a truck and come with you to pick up the animals, if you need help."

"I have two dogs already, but I can take two more," my dad added. "On a temporary basis," he emphasized.

"I can take a few also." Hazel jumped on the bandwagon.

"I admire what you're trying to do," Willa commented, "but it seems like you'll already have your hands full with Hometown Christmas. I realize that saving these animals is important to you, but the money we earn during our fund-raisers pays for our volunteer fire department and free public library, among other things. Hometown Christmas is the biggest event of the year."

"I can do both," I promised.

"What does everyone think?" Willa asked.

"I'm for the idea as long as we don't need the gym," Hazel said. "I'd just like to emphasize that if a conflict arises, the needs of Hometown Christmas should come first."

"Anyone disagree?" Willa asked.

No one spoke up.

"It looks like you have the committee's support," Willa decided. "As long as the gym isn't needed for Hometown Christmas, you're free to use it."

"Thank you."

"Okay, now let's go over the master calendar and then move on to new business."

I listened as Willa outlined plans for the community tree lighting on the sixth, the cookie exchange on the tenth, the opening of Santa's Village on the twelfth, the local theater company's performance of *White Christmas* on the thirteenth though the fifteenth, the last day of school before winter break and the opening of the kiddie carnival on the eighteenth, Hometown Christmas Spectacular on the nineteenth through twenty-second, the Holly Ball on the twenty-third, and the annual moonlight caroling and candlelight vigil on the twenty-fourth. Like I mentioned before, our little town tends to go just a little bit Christmas crazy.

Chapter 2

After the meeting, Charlie and I headed over to Zoe's Zoo. We entered the lobby, located at the front of the large log structure, which is shaped like a T. Beyond the lobby is a long hallway with offices, exam rooms, and housing for cats and small animals both wild and domestic. When you get to the end of the hall, you'll find facilities for dogs to the right, including kennels with individual indoor/outdoor runs and a large common area, and wild animals to the left. The wild animal facility is divided into both large and small enclosures. At the far end is the roomiest structure, which will be used to house larger wildlife. We are currently enlarging and updating this area in order to accommodate a greater number of our forest friends.

"Zak called," Jeremy informed me the minute I walked through the front door. "He wants you to call him back."

"Why didn't he just call my cell?" I asked the twenty-year-old expectant father as I picked up one of the cookies someone had left on the counter.

"He said he tried, but the call went right through to voice mail."

I looked at my phone, which I'd turned off the previous evening in order to conserve the rapidly dwindling battery and forgotten to turn back on. I don't know why this simple task is such a challenge for me. It's really pretty bad when you become known for something as ridiculous as your inability to keep your phone charged and activated.

"Okay, I'll call him. Anything else?"

"Elsa Black called. Her raccoons are back. She hoped you could stop by this afternoon and relocate them. She seemed distressed about the situation and mentioned that she needed it taken care of right away."

"Yeah, okay. I'll head over after I call Zak. These cookies are really good," I commented as I took a bite.

"Verna Green dropped them by as a thank you for helping her with the squirrels in her attic."

"They have a really unique flavor. What is that? Brandy?"

"Amaretto, actually."

"They're delicious. Remind me to get the recipe."

"Did you talk to the community group?" Jeremy asked.

I picked up a second cookie before answering. "I did, and we're good to go. As long as nothing goes wrong, we're free to use the gym, and most of the people on the committee agreed to temporarily house the dogs until we get them adopted."

"That's a relief. I checked with the county, and even though Zak paid to have our permits expedited, there's little hope we'll be able to open before the holiday. Still, it looks like things are on track. Sometimes I can't believe how well everything is working out. A few weeks ago things seemed pretty hopeless."

I knew what Jeremy meant. After losing my job, I'd settled into a deep depression that hadn't lifted until I'd been encouraged to take a temporary job at a turkey farm in the valley. I'd not only managed to save several hundred birds from holiday tables but solved a murder as well, my second in as many months. Perhaps if the Zoo didn't work out, I'd change careers and become a private investigator. Or not, I amended, as I looked around the building I loved and thought about all the animals whose lives I'd saved. Jeremy and I had a unique approach to animal rescue and adoption. We considered ourselves to be animal matchmakers who had a knack for placing those in our charge with just the right humans. Unlike many shelter adoptions, our success at maintaining long-term placements was nothing short of phenomenal.

"By the way," Jeremy added, "Pastor Dan asked me to help monitor and care for the animals they're borrowing for the live nativity. He somehow managed to secure a camel in addition to the donkey and sheep they always have."

"A camel? Wow. I hadn't heard."

"Gabe Turner is keeping it in his barn except for the hours the nativity is available for viewing. Ellie is in charge of lining up the town folk who have agreed to play the human roles, and she recommended they have someone on-site to keep an eye on the animals."

"Speaking of Ellie, she gave me this phone number to give to you." I handed Jeremy the number of Ellie's ex-boyfriend Rick's brother Rob, who was a single father and the founder of a single parent support group. Jeremy wasn't a father quite yet, but it wouldn't be long until he was going to need the support and services the group provided. I was still having a hard time wrapping my head around the idea that the dark-haired heavy metal drummer with a neck tattoo and nose ring was going to be a daddy, but in spite of Jeremy's rough exterior, I knew he was a good man with a kind heart who was going to make some little boy or girl a fantastic father.

"Thanks. Ellie said I was welcome to start attending support meetings right away. The gang invited me to join them for their weekly Sunday afternoon football gathering. I think I might go and get a start on meeting everyone. I have to admit that the closer the baby's birth gets, the more nervous I become."

"It's a big responsibility," I agreed. Jeremy's ex-girlfriend, Gina, wasn't ready to be a mother but had agreed to go through with the pregnancy if Jeremy raised the child and covered all her pre- and post-pregnancy expenses.

"Sometimes, when I'm home alone, I get this perfect clarity that lets me believe I've made the right choice and everything will be okay. But other times I wake up in a cold sweat, wondering how I'm going to take care of a baby on my own."

"You aren't alone," I pointed out. "You have friends who love you and will help and support you."

"I know." Jeremy smiled. "Ellie even volunteered to come and stay with us for the first few days after the baby comes home, while I figure out the whole feeding/changing schedule."

"Ellie's the best. And she knows what she's doing. She babysat all through high school, while I was messing around skiing on the mountain and boarding on the lake."

"That's one of the things Gina was upset about." Jeremy chuckled. "The doctor told her no skiing this winter."

"I have to admit I share her pain. It'd be a drag to miss a whole season. How's she feeling otherwise?"

"Pretty good, considering. She complains of being tired, but so far she's managed to avoid morning sickness."

"Is she still working?" Gina was a model.

"Actually, she is. She's so careful with her figure, she's barely gained any weight even though she's into her second trimester. Luckily, she's doing a catalogue for mountain wear and not bikinis."

"Is she showing at all?"

"A bit. It's really not noticeable unless you're really looking. I suppose it won't be long before she won't be able to work, though. I'm working on a budget so I can send her money during her time off, as well as pay the expenses. It's going to be tough."

"It'll be worth it," I encouraged.

"I know it will. I'm starting to get excited to be a dad. We're going to find out the baby's sex in a couple of weeks."

"Any preference?" I wondered.

"Not really. I think a boy might be easier, since I'm familiar with little boys and little boy needs, but a girl . . . a girl would be awesome. My own little princess."

"I'm sure that either way you'll be a great dad."

"I don't need to be a great dad. I just need to be a better dad than mine was to me."

I knew Jeremy's father had left him and his mom when he was young, and in many ways becoming a dad was bringing up issues he'd chosen not to deal with. His mom had died when he was a teenager and he had moved in with an elderly aunt who'd died two summers ago. I had to give Jeremy credit for his willingness to go the distance with his child. A lot of just-turned-twenty-year-old males would have taken the easy way out and let their girlfriends end their pregnancies, as Gina originally had intended to do.

When I had hired Jeremy two years ago, I'd thought of him as a nice kid with a lot of energy and a way with animals. Now I could see he'd matured into a man with a deep love for and commitment to his unborn child and a determination to leave his youth behind and become the father he'd always wished he'd had.

Chapter 3

After calling Zak and confirming his flight information for Friday afternoon, I headed over to Elsa Black's to deal with her raccoons. Elsa, a middle-aged woman with a hearty disposition and a rough exterior, lived with her equally rough-around-the-edges husband, Dilbert, on the east side of town. If I had to guess, I'd bet a week's wages that she'd yet to fix the door of her shed, as I'd instructed her to do the last time a raccoon family had decided to move in, causing hundreds of dollars of damage to the items they had stored there.

"Afternoon, Elsa," I greeted her as Charlie and I walked up her deeply rutted dirt drive.

"I'm afraid the raccoons are back," she informed me. "I hadn't even noticed until Billy Sherman's dogs started making a ruckus."

"Did you fix the door to the shed like I told you to the last time I was here?"

"I was going to, but I guess I never got around to it," Elsa admitted. "Seems like there are more chores to do than there are hours in the day."

"Yeah, I get that. This time, however, you might want to move the repair to the top of your list."

"I will," Elsa promised. "I'm glad you were able to come so quickly. Dilbert swore that if the little bandits broke into the shed again, he was going to shoot them dead."

Dilbert and Elsa lived on a large piece of property just outside the town limits. Dilbert is a nice enough guy, but I had no doubt that he'd follow through with his threat to kill the raccoon couple if I didn't remove them before he returned home. It wasn't that he was violent by nature; it was more that he was raised in a hunting family, and his relationship with the animals with which we share our habitat is vastly different than mine.

"I'll move the raccoons, then take Billy's dogs home. How long until Dilbert gets back?"

"'Bout an hour. Maybe more."

"Okay. I need to get my traps."

I had returned to my truck to get my equipment when Todd Miller, the Timberland County animal control worker who had been assigned my old route, arrived. The fact that Todd and I don't get along isn't surprising. I'm a rational individual with a keen instinct when it comes to dealing with problem animals, and Todd is a self-absorbed, egotistical idiot who barely knows a raccoon from a river otter.

"What are you doing here?" I asked the tall, blond-haired man with a fair complexion and a large head that reminded me of a Viking of old.

"Better question is, what are you doing here?"

"Elsa called me to take care of a raccoon problem."

Todd laughed. "Didn't you get the memo? Animal control is no longer your problem. Maybe you should pack up your toy box and head home."

"I'm simply here to help out a neighbor. Now, if you don't mind stepping aside," I said, continuing to unload my equipment, "I'm in a bit of a hurry."

"I'm thinking you should be the one stepping aside."

Todd was a good foot taller and outweighed me by at least a hundred and fifty pounds, so there wasn't a lot I was going to be able to do if he didn't voluntarily step aside. Still, hell would freeze over before I would step down, so it seemed we were at an impasse.

"Look," I tried again, "I brought everything I need to peacefully and calmly relocate the raccoons. I realize that domestic animal control is your jurisdiction, at least for now, but Sage and Queenie are good dogs that simply slipped away. I'll relocate the raccoons, then take the dogs home. It'll save you a pile of paperwork," I encouraged. "Besides, isn't the shelter in Bryton Lake already filled beyond capacity?"

"My job is to bring them in. It's up to the others to worry about what to do with them once they get there. You can deal with the raccoons, but I'm taking the dogs. It's against county ordinances to let your dog run free. I figure Mr. Sherman ought to pay the fine to get the mongrels back."

"I doubt Billy let his dogs run free," I argued. "Queenie is a tricky little thing; chances are she simply broke out of her pen and took Sage with her."

"You do that a lot when you worked this beat?" Todd asked. "Take dogs home without collecting the fines?"

"Occasionally," I admitted.

"Guess that's why I have a job and you don't." Todd snickered as he began rounding up the dogs. "I'm pretty sure this will be a second pickup for each of these dogs. Ol' Billy is going to have to take out a second mortgage on his house to get these mutts back."

Todd probably wasn't wrong. The county was tough on nuisance animals. The fine for a first offense was manageable, a second offense was painful, and a third was so steep that most folks left their dogs at the shelter for processing instead of paying it. I have to admit that while my dislike of Todd was personal, having to do with his noxious personality, there had always been a rivalry of sorts between the employees of the Bryton Lake shelter and me. The less-than-amiable working relationship mostly stems from a difference in philosophy. Bryton Lake is the capital of Timberland County, so the shelter there was considered the main facility even when the one here in Ashton Falls had been operating. As a general rule, ordinances regarding animal control originated in Bryton Lake and then were passed down to the satellite offices. The Timberland County Animal Shelter in Bryton Lake had established exceedingly rigid guidelines regarding leash laws and maximum durations of impounding.

Because of this differing approach to animal relocation and rehabilitation, I had been in a tug-of-war of sorts with the folks at Bryton Lake even before I was removed from my job. After the local shelter closed, the county had hired Todd to make a daily pilgrimage from the main facility into Ashton Falls to deal with domestic animal control. It killed me to know that quite a few dogs, many of which I'd placed with new owners in the first place, had spent time behind bars in the doggy jail located in the neighboring town. I guess it's not surprising that Todd resents my interference in what I'm sure he believes is his territory, but while animal control may be his job, Ashton Lake is my home. I will do whatever it takes to protect the four-legged creatures that live there.

I felt bad for Billy. I knew he was going to have a hard time paying the fine, and Todd the Toad was unlikely to give him a break due to financial hardship. Technically, Todd was following the dictates of the county ordinances I had been famous for ignoring entirely, but Ashton Falls wasn't anything like the larger, upscale town of Bryton Lake, and therefore, I believed, shouldn't have to adhere to their stringent laws.

After Todd left with the dogs, I relocated the raccoon couple, helped Elsa fix the door on the shed at least temporarily, then headed out into the woods to release the little troublemakers.

Chapter 4

After releasing the raccoons, Charlie and I headed over to Donovan's for a visit with my dad. Donovan's is a hybrid store offering a variety of products for the home and outdoors. Originally built by my grandfather over forty years earlier, the building is warm and cozy, with a seating area for social gatherings and an old-fashioned oak counter lined with jars of penny candy that still costs a penny.

"Hey, sweetheart. What brings you in on this stormy day?" Dad asked.

"Todd the Toad," I grumbled as I poured myself a cup of coffee from the pot my dad always kept on the counter.

"Up to his bad mojo again?"

"He picked up Billy Sherman's dogs," I informed him. "It'll be the second offense for each. I volunteered to take them home, but he was dead set on ruining poor Billy's life with the astronomical fine he's likely to get."

"Billy does seem to have a hard time keeping the dogs corralled. How many times did you pick them up and take them home before you were let go?"

"A bunch," I admitted.

"Maybe Billy needs to take a serious look at the amount of effort he's putting into keeping his dogs contained."

"I know you're right." I sighed. "Billy has a very relaxed approach to caging his dogs, and to be honest, it's probably my fault. I always took them home when they got out, so Billy learned that having them run free was no big deal."

"I guess he'll get the message now," Dad pointed out.

"Yeah, I guess."

"Maybe I can help Billy with some supplies to build a better pen," Dad offered.

I smiled. "Thanks, Dad. That would be great."

Kiva, the dog my dad adopted just over two months ago, wandered over from the seating area where he'd been sleeping next to my dad's retriever, Tucker. Originally, Kiva belonged to a local woman whose daughter had decided she needed to move to an assisted-care facility that didn't allow animals. The poor woman had been devastated until my dad agreed not only to adopt him but to take him down the mountain for a visit with her every couple of weeks.

"How is Mrs. Watson doing?" I asked.

"Better," Dad answered. "Kiva and I went for a visit the day after Thanksgiving. She seemed in good spirits, and she seems to like the staff at the facility."

"I'm glad to hear that. I was afraid she'd sink into a depression after having to leave Kiva behind. He was her baby."

"She misses him, but Kiva and I make the trip down to see her as often as we can. The staff has been really good about turning a blind eye to Kiva's presence."

I walked over to the seating area near the potbellied stove. Unlike in many of the larger stores in town, at Donovan's loitering was not only allowed, it was encouraged. I used to worry that my dad would go broke providing free coffee and doughnuts to the townspeople, who liked to settle in next to the warm fire and play a game or two of chess while they caught up on the local gossip. But Donovan's had been around for more than a generation and seemed to be thriving in spite of the changes that had come to our little town over the past forty years.

"What's this?" I picked up a copy from the stack of fliers my dad had left on the coffee table in front of the sofa.

"Sheriff Salinger came in today and asked me to pass those out. Toby Haskell is missing."

Toby was a ten-year-old boy from a troubled home who had run away on more than one occasion. "Do they think he ran away again?"

"The sheriff suspects he did, but they can't rule out foul play, so he's treating it as a possible kidnapping."

"Wow. How long has he been missing?"

"Since last week. He took his backpack and some of the clothes in his closet, so chances are he left of his own free will, but I told Salinger I'd pass out the fliers just in case."

I felt bad for the boy. His mother was a weak woman who had a tendency to hook up with abusive men. Toby had been removed from the home the previous summer, when it came to the attention of the folks from Child Protective Services that his mom's live-in lover had given Toby a black eye. I knew the mother had gotten counseling after her boyfriend was arrested and Toby had been returned to her. My gut told me things hadn't worked out and Toby had taken things into his own hands and run away. I hoped he was okay. Ten was young to be on your own, even if you were as intelligent and resourceful as Toby seemed to be.

I folded one of the fliers and put it in my back pocket. If Toby had run away, maybe I could track him down. After eight years working at the shelter, if there was one thing I was good at it was tracking down strays.

"Can you hand me that box of bows?" my dad asked.

I picked up the box, which was sitting open on the floor next to several other boxes of holiday garnish.

"I like your decorations, but where's the tree?" I asked as I carried it across the room.

He had strung pine garlands along the counter and was in the process of adding big red bows, but the tree that normally served as the focal point of his holiday display was noticeably absent.

"I haven't gotten around to putting it up yet," Dad admitted.

"How about we do it now? I'll help you."

My dad smiled. "I'd like that. It's been a while since we've put up the tree together. I'd better call Pappy. His feelings will be hurt if he's left out."

Pappy is my name for my grandfather, Luke Donovan.

"Call him," I instructed. "I'll run home, pick up Lambda, who's staying with me while Zak is away, and check on Maggie and the pups. I'll be back in thirty minutes."

******

By the time I'd returned with dogs in tow, Dad had brought in the tree and set it up in the alcove near the seating area. The tree was at least twelve feet in height, with closely placed branches and a wide and sturdy trunk. It was going to take a *lot* of lights to cover the thing, but when we were done, I knew it would be magical.

My dad, who is a good foot taller than I am, volunteered to climb the ladder and hang the lights. Pappy fed him the line while I was tasked with untangling them. Why is it that no matter how careful you are when storing the darn things, they still end up hopelessly tangled by the time you use them the following year?

After we finished with the lights, we began hanging the ornaments. My dad had a large box filled with every size, shape, and color imaginable. My favorite had always been the hand-carved forest animals Pappy had fashioned from bits of wood over the years.

"Do you remember when I made this ornament?" I asked my dad and grandfather. The ornament in question was a fairly decent replica of Santa Claus made out of cookie dough.

"Second grade," my dad replied. "I have no idea how that got in this box. I keep all the stuff you made at home for use on my personal tree."

"Embarrassed for it to be seen in public?" I teased.

"Afraid it will get stolen or broken," my dad corrected.

"If you saved all the masterpieces I made, you must have dozens of pinecone trees, cookie-cutter shapes, and photo holders. I'm pretty sure I made one of each every year until I reached the seventh grade."

"I kept and cherish every one," Dad confirmed.

"How about you, Pappy; did you save all of Dad's childhood creations?"

"Your grandma did," Pappy confirmed. "I'm not really sure what happened to all that stuff after she died. I suppose it's in the boxes in the attic. I haven't really bothered with a tree the past few years."

Pappy had stopped putting up a tree since my grandmother's death five years ago. He always joined my dad and me for Christmas dinner, but other than that, he kept pretty much to himself during the holiday season. I wasn't surprised that Christmas served as a painful reminder of the woman who had loved the season so much, but after five years it felt like it was time to rejoin the fun and festivities.

"I could use some help with the fund-raiser this year," I informed Pappy. "With the Zoo opening about the same time as Hometown Christmas, I think I'm going to have my hands full. I was hoping you'd be willing to serve as my co-chair."

"Anything for you, sweetheart. What do you need me to do?"

"Find me a Santa, for one thing. Earl Fielder is going to cover the Santa role for the tree lighting and Village opening, but he's already informed me that he's going to be out of town during Hometown Christmas."

"Where's old Earl going? He always plays Santa," Pappy said. Everyone in town knew that Earl not only *played* Santa, but in many ways, he *was* Santa. Not only was he a plump fellow who sported a long white beard, but he went out of his way to make sure everyone's Christmas wishes came true.

"I heard his wife is threatening to leave him if he doesn't go to her sister's farm in Minnesota this year. Most times she goes alone, but Earl said that this year she's been quite adamant."

"That's too bad. It won't be the same without Earl spreading his special brand of Christmas spirit."

"I'm not sure the Christmas spirit is what Earl will be spreading this year." I told them about his blowup at Rosie's that morning.

"He seemed okay when I came in," Dad commented.

"Gabe intervened and managed to calm him down. It's not like him to fly off the handle like that."

"Maybe his problems with Betty are a bit more serious than simply spending Christmas with her family," Pappy pointed out. "Marital problems can bring out the worst in a person."

"Maybe," I acknowledged. "Either way, I'm going to need a substitute Santa."

"I'm sure I can find someone," Pappy assured me. "Anything else I can help with?"

"Actually, I have a list. A long one. Maybe we can get together for lunch tomorrow and go over it."

"Rosie's at noon?"

"Sounds perfect."

******

After a couple of hours, Dad, Pappy, and I stood back to admire our handiwork. The tree was beautiful. It had grown dark while we worked, so Dad lit the tree and some candles and then turned off the lights. Soft Christmas jazz serenaded us in the background as we curled up on the sofa and told stories of Christmases past. At some point my dad ordered pizza and opened a bottle of wine. Between the three of us and the five dogs, we finished off two pizzas plus an order of bread sticks.

"I remember your first Christmas," my dad began as we sipped the last of the wine. "I was a new dad and so excited about starting new traditions. I took you into town and picked out your Christmas stocking, as well as a truckload of Santa gifts for under the tree."

"Grandma made you a red velvet dress to wear to church," Pappy added. "It had white lace and red bows. I remember it like it was yesterday."

"I kept that dress," Dad informed me. "Along with that first stocking and the stuffed puppy your mom sent you, which you dragged around the house until you were six."

"Mom gave me Mr. Floppy?" I asked. I remembered the puppy but assumed my dad had bought him for me.

"She did. She stopped by that first Christmas Eve. She couldn't stay, because her parents were waiting for her, but she wanted you to have the gift."

Suddenly I felt like crying. "Did she give me gifts other years?"

My dad hesitated. "A few. I was going to save this for later, but she sent us each a gift this year."

"She did?" I was shocked. "What is it?"

"Are you sure you don't want to wait until Christmas?" Dad asked.

"No, this is perfect. Let's open them now."

My dad went into the back room and returned with two huge boxes. Each contained the most awesome snowboards I'd ever seen.

"She bought us snowboards?" I was stunned. "They're so . . ." I searched for the right word. They were like no other boards I'd ever seen.

"They're prototypes," Dad supplied. "Your mom called me before she sent them. She's been staying with her parents in Switzerland while she tries to figure out her life, and she met a man who builds and sells snowboards and ski equipment. She talked him out of two of his boards and sent them to us. They are truly the first of their kind."

"Wow, that's so awesome. I can't wait to try mine out."

"Sunday," Dad suggested.

"It's a date."

Dad smiled.

"So how is Mom?" I had to ask. "I guess she didn't marry her prince?"

My mom had been in town a few months earlier, although no one had bothered to fill me in on her presence until after she'd left. After a lifetime of world travel, glamorous love affairs, and exotic adventures, she'd become engaged to a prince, only to realize at the last minute that marriage to a wealthy and powerful man she didn't love might not be all it was cracked up to be.

"No, she didn't get married. After she left here, she went to her parents' chalet and has been there ever since."

"And the guy who made the boards? Is he a new boyfriend?"

"She says they're just friends."

"Did she mention coming back for a visit? I didn't get to see her last time, and I thought maybe . . ."

"She didn't mention it specifically, but she did say that she misses us and has been thinking about us a lot lately. I imagine she'll come around after the holidays."

I know that most of you are going to find this ridiculous, given the number of times my mom has deserted my dad and me, but the knowledge that my mom didn't marry her prince and had in fact thought to send us gifts, filled me with a hope that, to most, would seem unwise and uncalled for. What can I say? Every year since I could talk, I've asked Santa to bring me my mother. While a snowboard from her isn't exactly what I wished for, it's still a lot. Apparently, when it comes to my mom, any hope, as little as it may be, is still hope.

Chapter 5

After a long and busy week, it was finally Friday. I tried to tell myself I was so jazzed because of the tree-lighting ceremony that evening, but the truth of the matter was, I'd missed Zak, and his plane would be landing in a few short hours at the airport in the valley. He'd left his car in long-term parking, so he didn't require a ride, but I'd talked to him the night before and he'd promised to pick me up in plenty of time for the annual event.

Our town has a long list of traditions. While most stem from our attempt to balance the budget, I feel like the tree lighting is something we do just for ourselves. The tree had been decorated for days now. Each evening, as I passed the park on the east end of town, I thought about how wonderful the same drive home from the shelter would be once the tree and the gazebo were lit. There would be a choir singing favorite carols as someone from the community was given the honor of lifting the switch and bringing Christmas spirit to our small town.

The ladies' auxiliary would sell hot cocoa and cookies, while the bars along the main drag would cater to those wishing for a more adult-type beverage.

Zak and I were meeting up with Ellie and Levi for a stroll along Main Street to view the shop windows, followed by a casual meal and a round of drinks at Mulligan's Bar and Grill.

I took Charlie, Maggie, and Lambda for a long run east along the lake trail, through the forest, and back along the beach, where the forest trail came out. I noticed a light on at Zak's lakefront estate as we passed it on our way to the boathouse. It was most likely the cleaning lady Zak had in once or twice a week, but on the off chance that Zak had returned early, I decided to jog around to the front to knock on the door.

"Can I help you?" The most beautiful woman I'd ever seen opened the door.

"My name is Zoe. I'm Zak's neighbor," I explained. "I saw the lights and thought he might be home."

"I'm afraid he isn't due to return until later this afternoon."

"Are you a friend?" I found myself asking.

"Something like that."

"Zak asked me to keep an eye on his house." This wasn't exactly a lie. Keeping an eye out for intruders was something neighbors often did for one another. "He didn't mention a visitor."

"I'm sure it just slipped his mind. I really do need to be going," the woman said, dismissing me. "I'll be sure to tell him you stopped by."

I thanked her and returned to the beach.

I couldn't help but wonder what the tall woman with silky blonde hair and eyes the color of a clear mountain morning was doing answering Zak's door. Not that I'm the jealous type, mind you. Because I'm not. And even if I were, I wouldn't be jealous of this particular woman because Zak and I are just friends, and if he wants to open his home to some gold-digging superbitch, who am I to stop him?

By the time I returned to the boathouse, showered, and changed into a dark green sweater and new pair of jeans, it had started to snow lightly. I took Charlie and Lambda with me and headed into town.

It was strange to spend the day at the shelter when there were no animals on-site. Jeremy and I, with the help of Zak, Levi, and Ellie, had scrubbed and painted the place from top to bottom. Before he left, Zak had ordered the construction of new pens that would allow us to house more large animals. Before the shelter closed, we had several bears, as well as a pair of coyote pups, in residence. Once word got out that we were qualified to deal with the rehabilitation and relocation of larger forest animals, shelters from all over the state had begun sending us their injured and orphaned wild animals. Needless to say, the demand had far exceeded our capacity, so when Zak purchased the shelter, we decided we would expand our efforts in that area.

"Oh good, you're here," Jeremy greeted me. "Earl Fielder was by looking for you. He came into town to pick up the Santa suit for the tree lighting tonight, but it wasn't in the storage closet at the community center like Hazel thought. Earl said Hazel remembered you were going to have it cleaned before storing it. They were hoping you knew where it might be."

I frowned as I tried to remember what I'd done with the outfit. I remembered taking it to the cleaners the week after Christmas the previous year. There had been a small tear in one of the seams, so I'd asked

Penelope Wentworth, the town seamstress, if she would be willing to mend it.

"I'm pretty sure the last I saw of it was when I dropped it off with Penelope," I informed Jeremy. "I'll call Hazel to see if she thought to check with her."

"Hopefully Penelope has it," Jeremy said. "Poor Earl is pretty stressed about not having the costume for tonight."

"It seems like Earl has been stressed in general the past few days," I commented.

"What do you mean?"

"He just seems to get all wigged out over the smallest things. I was in Rosie's a few days ago, and he threw a fit because he ordered his eggs over easy and they came out over medium."

"Seems odd. Earl is usually a pretty easygoing guy. I hope nothing is wrong. Most times easygoing folks don't turn into stress cadets unless they're dealing with a pretty big problem."

"It could be something to do with his wife," I speculated. "I know he's agreed to go to her family's this year, even though it means he'll need to turn his precious Santa suit over to someone else for Hometown Christmas."

"Yeah, that could be it. Everyone knows that women can make you crazy."

I threw a pen at Jeremy for his snide remark about the superior sex and then called Willa, who said she'd given the suit to the local theater company, who wanted to use if for her community-theater production of *Christmas in July*. I called the folks at the theater, who confirmed that they'd used it but had given it to my dad to use for the Holiday Faire, an arts-and-crafts fund-raiser that took place the weekend before Thanksgiving. So I called my dad, who confirmed that he'd dropped it off at the dry cleaner's, who'd promised to deliver it to Hazel in plenty of time for the tree-lighting ceremony.

I called Hazel again to tell her what the woman at the cleaner's had said, but she was certain she'd never received the costume, so I had to call the dry cleaner's again. This time I was told that the red-and-white costume had been picked up by Tawny Upton the previous day. This turn of events actually made sense, because Tawny is in charge of the tree lighting, so I called the preschool where Tawny worked and confirmed that she had the missing attire in the trunk of her car.

Tawny had planned to drop it off at Earl's, but her assistant hadn't come into work and she wondered if I might have time to deliver the package. I did, and promised her I'd be by shortly to pick it up.

******

Earl and Betty lived in a small but well-kept house in one of the older neighborhoods in town. The area was originally developed to provide housing for the seasonal laborers who worked in the old lumber mill back in the day when it was fully operational. After the mill closed, the small log cabins were sold off and updated to provide year-round residences.

"Who's there?" Betty called from behind the closed door.

"It's Zoe Donovan. I brought the Santa suit."

The door opened just an inch. I could see Betty peeking out from behind the structure, which was still secured with a chain. I waved to her, and she closed the door, removed the chain, and then opened the door the rest of the way.

"One never can be too careful," she explained.

I found Betty's behavior a little odd given the low crime rate in Ashton Falls, but I didn't say as much.

"I'm sorry for the inconvenience," I offered. "It seems the suit has made its way around town since last Christmas. Is Earl at home?"

"He's out. I'll take the getup."

I handed over the box with the freshly laundered suit. "I bet Earl is looking forward to the tree lighting tonight," I said, trying to make small talk. Normally Betty is the friendly type who always stops to chat when we meet.

"Yeah, I guess."

"It's nice that the weather is cooperating. Not like a few years ago, when we had that blizzard roll though and ruin the whole thing."

"Will there be anything else?"

"No, that's it. See you tonight?"

Betty closed the door without responding.

"Weird," I mumbled as I returned to my truck.

Betty's skittish behavior seemed odd at the least. The more I thought about it, the more I realized that there might be more going on with Earl and his wife than anyone realized. Not that Earl and Betty's relationship is my concern, but this is a small town, and part of living in a small town is that everyone makes it a point to know everyone else's business.

******

As the sun began its descent behind the mountain, I headed home to shower and change for the tree lighting. Anyone who knows me knows that I am a tomboy through and through, but every now and then, when the mood strikes, I find myself longing to be a real girl. Maybe it was the gently falling snow, the soft music, or the anticipation of seeing Zak for the first time in over a week, but I unwisely, as it turned out, decided to ditch the jeans and sturdy boots I'd planned to wear in favor of a new, tight red sweater, black leggings, and high-heeled boots I could barely walk in. I fashioned my hair into ringlets piled high atop my head and applied an uncharacteristically generous amount of makeup to my naturally freckled face.

I found myself looking out of the window as I waited in anticipation of Zak's arrival. He'd been gone just under six days, but it felt like forever. I busied myself opening a bottle of wine—the good kind Zak had brought over during a previous visit—lighting candles, dimming the lights, and stoking the fire. Christmas jazz played in the background and a full moon glistened on the nearby lake. I applied a spritz of perfume to my neck and gloss to my lips as Zak's truck pulled into the drive. My heart raced as he parked near the front door. I looked around at the scene I'd created and realized it looked like something out of the pages of a romance novel. An erotic romance novel.

"Oh God," I groaned. What was I thinking? This was Zak returning from a business trip, not some Prince Charming arriving on a white horse. I quickly blew out the candles and corked the wine, and was reaching out to turn up the lights when Zak knocked on the door, causing all three dogs to leap into action. I struggled to get my balance on my ridiculously high heels as I tripped over Lambda in the dark.

Zak opened the door just as I fell into a potted plant, which plummeted off the counter and onto my head.

"Are you okay?" Zak hurried to my side. He pulled me onto my feet as the dogs jumped around us, demanding his attention. Not only did I have soil from the plant down the front of my sweater but I had *wet* soil, since I'd watered just that day.

"I'm fine." Why is it that the earth never opens up and swallows you when you most need it to?

"What happened?" Zak started to laugh as he handed me a clean dishtowel. Not only was there wet soil on my sweater but apparently, based on Zak's amused expression, I had quite a bit of the muck in my hair as well.

"I made the mistake of getting between the dogs and the front door."

"Why is it so dark in here?"

I blushed, thanking the powers that be that it *was* dark so Zak was unlikely to notice. "I was upstairs getting ready," I lied. "I was just about to turn on some lights down here when you knocked on the door, sending the dogs into a frenzy."

Zak took the towel from my hand and wiped a streak of grime from my cheek. "I missed you." He kissed me gently on the lips.

I wanted to say that I'd missed him, too, but was unable to speak.

"Go upstairs and get washed up. I'll clean up the mess down here."

I walked toward the stairs, willing my shaky legs not to give way.

"And Zoe . . ."

"Yeah?"

"It's snowing outside. Perhaps you should wear your boots with the flat heel and rubber sole."

I scampered up the stairs like the devil himself was chasing me. I quickly showered and changed into a heavy wool sweater, worn jeans, and my sturdy boots. I decided to forgo the makeup and styled hair in favor of the natural look I normally sported. Then I grabbed my heavy jacket and headed back down the stairs, feeling less like a sex kitten and more like plain old Zoe.

Chapter 6

As they do every year, pretty much everyone in town came out for the tree-lighting celebration. The temperature had dropped during the past few days, hinting at the cold winter days ahead. Zak and Levi sandwiched Ellie and me in between them, providing welcome heat as we struggled to stay warm.

The mayor gave a short speech, followed by carols performed by the high-school choir and the flipping of the switch that provided power to both the tree and the lights covering the gazebo. Everyone cheered as Ashton Falls' season of Christmas crazy officially began.

"It looks like Earl is back to his old self," I observed.

"Yeah, he seems as jolly and lively as ever," Ellie agreed. "He stopped in at Rosie's today, and he was a total basket case. I don't think I've ever seen him quite so irritable and agitated."

"I know he was upset he couldn't find the suit," I said as the choir began a holiday medley to which most of the town joined in.

"No, it was more than that," Ellie said over the noise. "If I had to guess, looking for the suit was little more than a distraction from what was really bothering him. Mom said he and Betty have been having some problems. In fact, I overheard several people mentioning that Betty is seriously thinking about staying with her family rather than returning after the holiday."

"Poor Earl," I sympathized. "I've heard there are problems in paradise, but they've always been so good together."

"I'm sure they'll work it out," Levi inserted. "Still, it's not going to be the same, not having the *real* Santa here for the bulk of the Christmas season."

"The real Santa?" Ellie laughed.

"Earl *is* the real Santa," Levi defended. "He not only listens to the Christmas wishes of the local children but he makes sure they come true."

I had to agree with Levi. Earl was as close to the real thing as it got. Not only did he look the part, but most times he lived his life as a jolly elf who volunteered at the local elementary school and read to children at the library. Earl and Betty had never had children, but Earl frequently commented that the children of Ashton Falls were all his kids in a roundabout sort of way.

"He did buy seven bikes for kids from underprivileged families last year," Levi pointed out.

"Yeah, and two years ago, when Freddie Waters shared a secret with Santa, revealing that his family was on the verge of being kicked out of their home after Mr. Waters lost his job, Earl not only helped negotiate a refinance but paid the fees as well," I added.

"Okay," Ellie conceded. "I guess Earl *is* the real Santa. I know I really believed he was when I was a kid. One year I told him, and only him, that I wanted a Little Miss Manners doll, and it was under the tree when I woke up."

"Little Miss Manners?" Levi teased.

"It was a popular doll in its day," Ellie said, defending herself.

Levi rolled his eyes as the speeches from local businesspeople commenced.

After the speeches had been delivered and all the carols had been sung, Zak, Levi, Ellie, and I headed to Mulligan's for some adult refreshment. Mulligan's is a bar first and foremost and a restaurant as an afterthought. They specialize in what most people think of as bar food: an assortment of pizza, sandwiches, and appetizers. We ordered pizza and chicken wings, along with a couple of pitchers of our favorite beer.

"It was a nice tree lighting, but not the best one ever," Levi commented. "Personally, I think the elves Tanner Brown came up with three years ago added a great deal to the event."

Levi was referring to the two women we'd all come to think of as the Hefner elves, given the fact that they looked like someone Hugh himself would hang out with.

"Speaking of the Hefner elves, I ran into Kendra a couple of weeks ago," Ellie said.

For those of you who are wondering, Ellie is referring to Kendra Knight, Tanner's niece, and not

Kendra Wilkinson, the *real* Hefner "elf," although they look remarkably alike.

"She mentioned that Tanner was selling his boat and moving off the mountain."

"Really?" Tanner Brown is a crusty old fishing boat captain who attends the book club I frequent every Thursday night. "It's odd he hasn't mentioned it."

"Kendra said he's been having problems with a couple of the other charter companies, and after giving it a lot of thought decided a long, drawn-out battle wasn't something he was interested in."

"Tanner doesn't seem like the type to back down to me," Levi mused.

"He's getting on in years," Zak pointed out. "Maybe he was ready to hang up his fishing pole anyway."

"The way Kendra made it sound, there's already been quite a bit of sabotage going on behind the scenes. Apparently, Tanner found his hull full of water a few weeks ago and had to cancel his bookings for three days while he fixed the breach," Ellie supplied.

"Does Tanner know who did it?" I wondered.

Ellie shrugged. "Probably, but Kendra didn't say. All she really told me was that Tanner was done with the whole thing. He's moving to Arizona after the first of the year."

I'd miss the crusty old guy, but I didn't really blame him for not wanting to get caught up in a battle of one-upmanship. I thought about Earl and his trouble, and Tanner and his. It made me feel bad to think that friends and neighbors were going through rough times. It seemed like the Christmas spirit was failing to make quite the impression it normally did. But the great thing about Christmas magic is, it usually comes around just when you need it the most.

"I could use your help with a project," I said to Ellie.

"What kind of project?"

"I had dinner the other night with my dad and Pappy. We decorated the tree Dad got for Donovan's, and we started talking about Christmases in the past. It's been five years since my grandma died, and it occurred to me it might be time to resume some of the traditions we left behind. I want to make my grandma's Christmas Eve soup, but I don't have the recipe. You've had the soup on more than one occasion and you know your way around a kitchen, so I was hoping you could help me figure things out."

"You mean the potato cheese soup?"

"Yeah, the one she served in bread bowls."

Ellie paused. "Yeah, I think I can help you figure it out. I know it had potatoes, leeks, cream, and cheese. I assume it was cooked in a chicken-broth base. I'll make a test batch; we can taste it and take it from there."

I smiled. Pappy would be so surprised if I made Grandma's soup to serve at Christmas dinner. I knew the traditional dish would brighten his day and bring some of the magic back to his favorite holiday.

Chapter 7

I woke up on the morning of December 13 with a huge smile on my face. Although I do tend to be a bit superstitious, not even the lore surrounding the curse of Friday falling on the thirteenth day of the month could put a damper on my optimism. I was more than halfway through the Christmas crazy events and everything was right on schedule.

The weekend after the tree lighting, I'd dug into the final preparations for Hometown Christmas. The vendors had been contacted, the contracts signed, the carolers lined up, the decorations hung, and the sleigh team readied. And not only had I totally nailed the planning and preparation phase of the important fund-raiser, but along the way, I'd managed to bake ten dozen cookies for the cookie exchange.

The icing on the cake was the fact that Santa's Village had opened the day before, to long lines of happy kids and harried parents. Earl Fielder was a killer Santa, as usual, and I was sorry he was going to miss the final week of the season. Still, Pappy had grudgingly agreed to fill in when he was unsuccessful in his campaign to find a substitute, and I suspected that a little forced Christmas jolly was exactly what he needed to once again embrace the holiday my grandmother had loved so much.

I climbed out of bed and slipped into heavy jeans and a sweatshirt. It had snowed for the past three days, and the dogs and I were anxious to get out of the house. After feeding everyone and checking on the pups, Charlie, Maggie, and I headed out to the beach for a sunrise snowshoe.

It's always really beautiful the morning after a snow. The trees hung heavy with their burden, while the squirrels and coyotes made tracks in the unmarred snow. For anyone who has never experienced the silence of a winter morning high atop an isolated mountain, it's an awesome event that's hard to describe. I stood on the edge of the waterline and looked out over the lake, then closed my eyes and listened; the only sound was that of my own breath.

As the sun peeked over the distant summit, the dogs and I headed down the beach. We'd received almost four feet of snow during the past week, making trudging through the fresh powder a bit of a workout, which, I'll admit, was sorely needed. I knew that the likelihood of running into one of our larger forest animals was slim, but still I watched for what can only be described as a magical sight. The mule deer that frequent the area regularly move to the valley floor, where there is less snow during the winter months, and our resident bears are normally deep in slumber this late in the year. But every now and then, when the moment is just right, I've come across a straggler on my morning walks.

After returning to the boathouse, I poured myself a cup of coffee, then headed into my cozy bathroom for a long, hot shower. I knew the following week would be a busy one, and I used this quiet time to prepare mentally. I finished my shower, dressed warmly, dried my hair, and was just about to make a light breakfast—pancakes and bacon—when there was a knock on the door. It was Zak, with Lambda at his side.

"Sorry to drop by so early," he apologized. "I tried calling, but your cell phone was off."

Of course it was.

"I'm afraid there's a problem with the software I've been hired to develop and we need to head to the national office right away. Can Lambda stay with you?"

"Of course," I said. *We?* I thought. "You know Lambda is always welcome. I hope the problem is nothing serious."

I looked around Zak's chiseled chest toward his truck, where I spied the woman—who, I'd discovered, was none other than his much-too-beautiful business partner—waiting in the passenger seat. She glared at me as she pointed to her watch. Apparently, my witty banter was making them late.

"Nothing I can't fix," Zak assured me.

I turned my attention to him and smiled. I reached up to hug him, knowing that the witch in the truck would be watching.

"I'll miss you," I cooed.

Zak looked surprised but smiled. "I'll miss you, too. I was going to bring this up later, but now that I'm leaving . . ."

"Bring what up?" I asked, sweet as pie.

The demon in the truck honked the horn. I kept smiling and brushed an imaginary hair from Zak's chest. Zak must have caught on to what I was doing, because he glanced at the woman behind him and grinned. This is going to sound utterly ridiculous, but I can't tell you how happy it made me that Zak realized I was jealous and liked it.

"I wanted to ask if you wanted to go to the Holly Ball with me."

"Like a date?" I asked.

"If you'd like."

"I'd love to." I smiled.

Zak pulled me into his arms and kissed me. The kiss was . . . the kiss was wonderful. No, wonderful is too tame a word. The kiss was life changing. I couldn't help but glance at the woman in the truck as Zak turned to leave.

"Don't worry," Zak assured me. "Belinda is an associate, nothing more. I'll call you every night."

I felt marginally better.

******

From that point on, the day went downhill. I arrived at the Zoo with Charlie and Lambda on my heels only to find Jeremy up in arms over whatever it was he was reading.

"I have news."

"Good or bad?" I asked.

"Bad. They've put a hold on our permit."

"What?"

"It seems someone from the county has challenged our right to compete with their program."

"Compete? Are they insane? The Bryton Lake facility is bursting at the seams and someone is afraid we might lighten that load?"

"I don't think the complaint came from the people at the shelter. My bet is that a number cruncher who has never even visited the shelter or been exposed to the animals noticed that between the reduction in expense after our shelter closed and the increase in revenue due to Todd the Toad's aggressive leash control, the numbers are looking pretty good." Jeremy handed me the letter he'd been reading.

I was tempted to call Zak but knew he had his own problems. Besides, after the kiss this morning, I didn't want to be seen as incompetent or needy.

"It says there's a hearing scheduled after the first of the year. Our permit has been delayed until after that meeting. This really is bad news."

"There's more," Jeremy hedged.

"More good or more bad?"

"It depends. One of the dogs rescued in the puppy-mill scheme six weeks ago was reunited with its family."

"They gave the dog back to the mill owner?"

"No, its real family. It turns out that some of the dogs were stolen from loving families and brought to the mill to reproduce. One of the families never stopped looking. They wandered into the Bryton Lake shelter and saw a photo of their missing pet. The dog had been chipped, so ownership was confirmed, and dog and family were reunited."

"That's wonderful."

"Yeah, well . . ."

I began to get a queasy feeling in the pit of my stomach when Jeremy wouldn't look me in the eye.

"After the county found out that dog was stolen, they decided to check all the dogs for previous owners. They're coming by to check Maggie later this morning. They think she fits the description of a dog that went missing back in August."

My heart sank. I'm a huge advocate for reuniting dogs with their families, but during the time Maggie had lived with me, she had become part of my family. I knew it was procedure to check missing-dog reports when taking in a stray, but since the dogs in question had come from an abusive owner and not from the streets, this very important step had been overlooked.

"What time will they be here?"

"In an hour or so. If you want to bring Maggie down, I can oversee the meeting."

"No. Send whoever shows up to the house. I'll take Charlie with me but leave Lambda with you. I'll come by for him after I meet with the shelter people."

"Okay, if you're sure."

"I'm sure."

Suddenly my perfect day was turning into an endless nightmare.

******

During the next hour, as I waited for the county to arrive, I sat on the floor of my bedroom with Maggie and her four pups. I tried to reconcile myself to the fact that Maggie might have a family who loved and missed her. I reminded myself how devastated I'd be if Charlie should turn up missing, and how much I'd hope that whoever found him returned him to me.

While my mind accepted the situation, my heart was breaking. I thought about how Maggie jumped into my arms as I returned home every night, and how she licked my face every morning as I struggled to wake up and face the day. I tried to suppress the tears that were streaming down my face as I held the little dog on my lap for what I knew could very well be the last time.

As my tears turned into a sob, Charlie began to whine. He sat down next to me and put his paw on my knee. Charlie always has been sensitive to my moods, and I'm sure my obvious despair while holding Maggie was confusing him. "It's okay. I'm okay," I assured him.

He licked the tears from my face, then laid down and put his head in my lap. Maggie settled on the other side, and I leaned against the wall behind me. I embraced the few minutes I had left with my family, longing for the moment to never end.

I took a deep breath and prayed for strength when I heard the knock on the boathouse door. I ordered Maggie and Charlie to stay upstairs in the loft as I wiped the tears from my face and made my way slowly downstairs. I opened the door to find not only one of the employees of the Bryton Lake shelter but a well-dressed woman and a young girl of about ten as well. The girl was tall and thin, with long black hair that brushed her waist and a hopeful expression in her deep green eyes.

"This is Jackie Lawson and her daughter Hilary," the woman from the shelter introduced. "They're the ones who reported a missing dog back in August."

"Is Sasha here?" the little girl asked.

"Let's find out." I tried to put on a brave face as I forced a smile. "Maggie," I called.

Maggie came running down the stairs, with Charlie close behind. When she saw Hilary, she increased her speed and jumped straight into the girl's arms. In all the time I'd had her, I'd never seen her quite so happy. Hilary cried as Maggie, or I guess it was Sasha, licked her face.

"We're prepared to run the chip to prove ownership," the woman from Bryton Lake stated.

"No need." I wiped away the tears that were streaming down my face. "It looks like Maggie has found her family. Both of you," I gestured toward Hilary and her mother, "please come in and have a seat. We need to discuss the puppies."

I explained to the woman, who turned out to be very nice and extremely understanding and sympathetic to my plight, that I'd already promised the puppies to members of the community when they were old enough to be weaned. Jackie assured me that she'd honor my commitments and contact the prospective puppy owners in the next week or so. Somehow I managed to keep the bulk of my emotions at bay until Hilary and her mother left with Maggie and her pups. Tears streamed down my face as I watched the dogs drive away. Maggie had only been with me for six weeks, but during that time I'd grown to love her so, so much. I knew that returning her to the little girl who loved her was the right thing to do, but the truth of the matter is that often times, doing the right thing can hurt so darn much.

Chapter 8

By the time I arrived at the community center for Santa's Village, I figured the day couldn't get any worse. Maggie was gone from my life forever, even though a small part of me realized this was actually a good thing, and Zak was *God knew where* with his beautiful and manipulative assistant. (I actually didn't know if she was manipulative, but she looked like she would be.) The highly anticipated opening of Zoe's Zoo would be delayed at least a month, maybe more, and the snow that had seemed so beautiful just that morning had turned into a strategic nightmare as hundreds of tourists arrived for the weekend.

"Don't you love all this snow?" Ellie, who was seasonally dressed in a Santa hat and red sweater, asked as she joined me near the Santa house.

I turned and growled. At least I felt like growling. The reality is, I most likely groaned.

"Someone woke up on the wrong side of the bed this morning," Ellie teased.

"I woke up on the right side. It's everything that's happened since that's the problem."

I took Ellie step-by-step through the nightmare that had been my day.

I felt like crying when Ellie gave me one of her long, hard Ellie hugs. "I'm so sorry about Maggie," she said, squeezing me tightly. "I know you loved her."

"You should have seen how happy she was when she first caught sight of Hilary."

Ellie handed me a tissue. "You saved Maggie's life," she reminded me. "Without you, Hilary and Maggie would never have found each other. You should feel good about that."

"I do." I dried my eyes and smiled. "I guess moments like this are why I do what I do."

"And you do it better than anyone else. It's a drag about the permit."

"It'll set us back at least a month. I can't believe the county is doing this. I just hope Zak can get this fixed when he gets back into town. If he comes back, after spending the week with his beautiful partner," I said, sulking.

Ellie laughed. "I see why you're so upset about the permit, but you're an idiot to worry about Zak. He's rich and handsome. He could have any girl he wanted."

"And that's supposed to make me feel better?"

"My point is that Zak has beautiful women throwing themselves at him all the time."

"Has anyone ever told you that you're really bad at this cheering up thing?"

Ellie laughed again. "On numerous occasions. What I'm trying to get to is the fact that Zak isn't going to be swayed by a pretty package or a flirty, come-hither look. He likes you. I've seen the way he looks at you. The way he's *always* looked at you, even when you were too busy hating him to notice. Zoe Donovan, if there's one thing you don't have to worry about, it's Zak's devotion to you."

I wanted to believe Ellie. I really did, but I was having a hard time bringing jealous Zoe to heel.

"I made the test batch of soup." Ellie changed the subject. "It's in the kitchen, if you want to try it."

"You brought it with you?"

"Sure, why not? I figured you'd be here, and the kitchen has both a refrigerator and a microwave."

"Great. Let's see how it turned out."

"I have to warn you," Ellie began as we walked into the kitchen, "it's a place to start, but it isn't your grandma's recipe. At least not yet. We'll taste it, see if we can figure out what might be missing, and take it from there."

"Okay."

Ellie took the bowl out of the refrigerator and heated the soup in the microwave. She gave me a spoon and I took a bite. The thick and creamy soup was good, but not as good as Grandma's.

"I think Grandma's was cheesier."

"Yeah, that's what I thought, too," Ellie agreed. "I'm going to add in some Parmesan and maybe some jack with the cheddar for the next batch. Anything else?"

I tasted it again. "I'm not sure. Grandma's soup had a distinct taste, but I'm not sure exactly what it was. Maybe once you add the additional cheese . . ."

"Okay. I'll make another batch and we'll taste it again."

"It's nice of you to go to all this trouble."

"No trouble at all. I love developing recipes. It's like a treasure hunt, trying to find just the right ingredients to make a good dish into a spectacular one."

"You're a lot like my grandma," I commented. "She loved to mess around in the kitchen, trying to come up with new and unusual recipes. I only wish she had written things down. Even when people asked her what was in a dish, she'd usually respond with 'a little of this and a little of that.'"

"I promise you, I'm writing everything down as I work on this," Ellie assured me.

"Zoe," Hazel Hampton interrupted us, "have you heard from Earl?"

"Isn't he supposed to be here?"

Santa's Village was due to open in less than twenty minutes. Earl normally arrived a good hour early.

"He hasn't shown up, and he isn't answering either his cell or his home phone. There are a good thirty kids in line. They'll be so disappointed if Santa doesn't come."

"I'll call Pappy." My grandfather would be covering for Earl beginning next Thursday, and he'd already rented a costume to fit his tall, thin frame, which in no way resembled Earl's short and stout one.

Pappy answered on the first ring. He promised to come straight over, but after twenty minutes he still hadn't arrived. I was beginning to worry about him, but the more urgent matter at hand seemed to be the revolting kids and angry parents. Many had been waiting in line for over an hour.

"Pappy left his Santa suit in the storage room. We just need a warm body that will fit into it," I told Ellie.

I looked around the room. Tanner Brown was about the right weight, although he was shorter than Pappy. He'd make a grumpy Santa, but beggars can't be choosers. I put on my most persuasive persona and charmed—okay, bribed—Tanner into filling in until Pappy arrived. Luckily, Penelope was on-site and agreed to make a few quick alterations so the suit wouldn't drag on the floor when Tanner walked.

******

Four hours later, the crowds had left, the community center was deserted, and neither Earl nor Pappy had ever called in or shown up.

"You can leave the costume in the back room where you changed," I instructed Tanner as I handed him the Franklin I'd promised.

"I'm starting to think I should ask for more," Tanner grumbled as he stared at the hundred-dollar bill. "You said I'd only have to do it until your grandpa showed up."

"I know. I'm sorry. I don't know what happened to him. How about I bring you some of my famous snowball cookies?"

"Well . . ." Tanner hesitated. "Okay."

I sighed in relief.

"By the way, you better have that suit cleaned," Tanner warned me. "Some snot-nosed kid peed on me."

"Thanks for letting me know."

"Guess I'll head back and change. Don't forget the cookies."

"I'll bring them to book club." I had frozen part of each of the three types I'd baked for the cookie exchange, so I was in good shape there.

Hazel, Ellie, and a few other members of the events committee helped clean up while I continued to call Pappy. I was just about to call out the National Guard when he arrived, looking more harried than I'd ever seen him.

"What happened?" I asked.

"Accident outside of town. The road was totally blocked and the tow trucks were backed up with all the snow. Took hours for one to arrive."

"Why didn't you call me?" I scolded. "I was worried something horrible had happened to you."

"Phone was dead."

So that's where I get it.

"I'm just glad you're okay. I still haven't heard from Earl."

"I'm afraid he was the victim of the accident," Pappy informed me.

"Is he okay?"

"Hard to tell. An ambulance came by just as I got there. I know they rushed him to the hospital."

I hugged my pappy, glad that he hadn't been injured, as I'd been imagining. "You're soaking wet. Go home and get warmed up."

"Okay. I'll see you tomorrow?"

"Count on it."

I watched Pappy walk away. He was slowing down in his old age, and I worried about him. He'd been one of the constants in my life and I wasn't sure what I'd do if anything happened to him.

"Everything is locked up," Hazel informed me. "Guess I'll head on home."

"Okay. I'll see you tomorrow."

"Want to get a bite to eat?" Ellie asked. "I'm starving." Ellie was tall and thin, with a quick metabolism and a voracious appetite that never seemed satisfied. "I had a big lunch, but all this Christmas jolly really works up an appetite."

"Sounds good. I just need to get the Santa suit so I can drop if off at the cleaner's."

"I got a ride over with Mom, so I'll just go with you, if you can drop me at home after."

"Sounds like a plan."

"Hell of a day," Ellie commented as we walked toward the back room.

"Tell me about it. It started off so good and went downhill from there."

"At least it can only get better," Ellie encouraged.

"Don't say that," I warned. "Every time someone says that, things get worse."

"Sorry." Ellie laughed.

"Tanner," I called, knocking on the closed door. I figured he'd be long gone by now, but I thought it wise to check. When no one answered, I opened the door.

"Tanner!" I ran forward. "Call nine-one-one," I told Ellie. "It's Tanner. I think he's dead."

Chapter 9

An hour later, Ellie, Levi, and I sat in Mulligan's, nursing our drinks. Ellie had called Levi while I spoke to Sheriff Salinger, and he'd agreed to meet us at the bar as soon as our interview was over. One of the best things about having a regular hangout is that, even in the midst of turmoil, there's something comforting about the familiarity that can be found in your favorite booth, with your best friends, and go-to comfort food.

"Salinger is going to get suspicious if you keep finding all these dead bodies," Levi joked as he dipped a crispy onion ring into a puddle of ketchup.

"I think he already is. His line of questioning felt more like an inquisition."

"At least I have an alibi this time," Levi stated. Last October, Levi had spent a night in jail before we were able to prove he was innocent of an eerily similar murder.

"Poor Tanner most likely never saw what hit him." Ellie sighed as she pushed her food around on her plate.

"Did it look like there had been a struggle?" Levi wondered.

"No. Someone must have been waiting for him," Ellie speculated. "He never even got a chance to change out of his Santa suit."

The Santa suit. I made a mental note to call Earl to see if he was out of the hospital and able to play Santa the following day. If not, I'd need to talk to Betty to see about borrowing Earl's suit for Pappy to use until we could make other arrangements. It'd be too short and too big, but we didn't have much of a choice. I'd also need to call Pappy to give him a heads-up that he might be needed to man Santa's Village the following day.

"Did Salinger have any idea who might have done it?" Levi asked.

"Not that he said," Ellie answered. "I can't imagine why *anyone* would want to kill Tanner."

I pulled a notepad out of my purse and jotted down a few to-dos while Levi and Ellie continued to talk. It wasn't that I was unaffected by Tanner's death, but my way of coping with unpleasant news has always been to throw myself into some urgent task that occupied my mind as well as my emotions.

"He was a crusty sort," Levi pointed out. "Maybe he pissed off the wrong guy."

"Someone would have to be pretty mad to bash in the guy's head," Ellie argued. "Tanner is a curmudgeon, but he's *our* curmudgeon. Most folks in town liked and respected him in spite of his rough exterior."

Levi nodded. "I'm going to miss the old guy."

"I'm glad none of the kids wandered in to the back room." Ellie shivered. "Seeing Santa dead like that. There was so much blood. We're never going to get the suit cleaned in time for tomorrow's Village."

"I wouldn't worry about that. I heard that Sheriff Salinger has taped off the entire building," Levi said. "One of the detectives who came up from the county office told me they'll most likely keep the building closed until they complete their investigation."

"What?" I joined the conversation. If the community center was going to be closed, they'd need the gym for Hometown Christmas and the pet adoption event, which I'd been advertising heavily, would end up getting canceled. I hated myself for being concerned about the darn event after what had happened to someone I'd known since I was a little girl, but the lives of so many animals were depending on it.

"One of the guys on my softball team works in the sheriff's office," Levi said. "He came in to pick up some takeout while you girls were in the ladies' room. I asked him about the murder, and he mentioned that the community center is going to be closed until further notice. I guess they need to get their techs in to check for fingerprints and stuff."

"Fingerprints? It's a *community* center," I emphasized. "Salinger is probably going to find prints for everyone in town."

"Yeah, but not everyone was in the room where Tanner was killed," Levi pointed out. "Besides, I think they're looking for evidence other than prints."

"If they close the center, we'll have to move the Hometown Christmas events."

"Maybe Salinger will figure things out quick." Ellie tried to sound optimistic.

I rolled my eyes in a dramatic gesture meant to convey my lack of faith in our good sheriff. If there's one thing you can count on with Salinger, it's that he'll act in a contradictory and ineffective way as he approaches the task of finding Tanner's killer.

"You're going to investigate," Ellie realized.

"Someone has to."

"You know what happened last time," she warned.

"The guy can't get me fired from a job I no longer have," I pointed out.

"No, but he can speak out against the permit you so desperately need."

I looked at Ellie. She was right. Getting involved was both impulsive and stupid. Of course, I've never been known for being anything other than impulsive, and stupid . . . well, I guess that's a matter of opinion.

"We need to work fast," I said. "The vendors will be here to set up for Hometown Christmas next Wednesday. If the community center is still closed then, we'll have to have them set up in the gym. The pet adoption clinic will have to be canceled, and dozens of animals will die."

"Are you sure about this?" Levi asked. "Ellie is right, you know. Getting involved could put your permit at risk. Maybe you could have the pet adoption in the park."

"With all the snow we've been having?"

"I'm sure there must be somewhere," Ellie encouraged.

"How about we cross that bridge when we come to it? In the meantime, let's see what we can do about getting the murder solved and the community center open."

"I'm in," Ellie stated.

"Me, too," Levi agreed.

"So where do we start?" Ellie asked.

"We need to make a list of everyone who might want Tanner dead."

"Well," Ellie said, "he was going to sell his boat and move over a conflict he had with some of the other charter companies. I'd say that's as good a place as any to start."

"My pappy was pretty close with Tanner. I'll see if I can come up with a list of exactly who Tanner had a beef with," I offered.

"I know a guy who works for one of his competitors," Levi offered. "It seems there's always been a friendly sort of competition between the fishing charters in the area, but things really heated up when a new company came to the lake last summer. I think they work out of the south shore but frequented locations known for good fishing on the north shore."

"Do you know the name of the new company?" I asked.

"Yeah, I made a note of it." Levi took out his phone and skimmed his notes until he found the entry he was looking for. "Get Hooked Charters. The owner's name is Gilbert French. I heard he used to do deep-sea charters but decided to retire to the lake, so he sold his bigger boat and bought a totally tricked out fishing boat."

"Tricked out?" I asked.

"The boat has all the bells and whistles. I hate to admit it, but the reason I had the guy's info to begin with was because I'd heard how successful he's been. In my opinion, he has the potential to put the old-school fishing boats out of business."

"I don't get it." I frowned. "If this guy has the kind of money it must take to outfit a boat in the manner you describe, why work our little lake?"

"I guess there's a lot of money to be made in tourism."

"But if this guy is doing so well, why would he mess with Tanner's boat?" Ellie asked.

"It really doesn't track that he would," I agreed. "Still, I suppose we should put this guy on the list. Wouldn't hurt to nose around a bit."

"I'll see what I can find out," Levi offered. "And I'll talk to some of the other charter boat captains as well."

"I'll talk to Tanner's ex-wife," Ellie said. "If there was ever anyone with motive to off the guy, it's probably her."

"Okay. I'll see what I can find out from his friends: Pappy and the book-club gang for a start. We'll meet tomorrow and compare notes."

Chapter 10

Saturday promised to be a sunny day with unseasonably warm temperatures. I decided to strap on my cross-country skis and head to the hilly trail behind the boathouse to work off some steam. I'd lain awake most of the night, not analyzing Tanner's murder and our list of suspects as I should have, but rather wondering why Zak had never called as he'd promised. I'd checked to make certain my phone was turned on at least a dozen times. I know Zak and I aren't really a thing, and his comment that he'd call every night might not have meant *every* night, but that didn't keep thoughts of Zak tangled up with Belinda's voluptuous body at bay.

As I headed out of the door with Charlie and Lambda on my heel, I promised myself that I'd put all thoughts of Zak and his potentially torrid love affair out of my mind. Please understand that I realized I was being completely ridiculous. I'd spent most of the night trying to reason with myself. My mind told me that just because Zak had worked with the beautiful Belinda for lord knew how long, and just because she was staying at his house while she was in town, it didn't mean they were sleeping together. Zak is a businessman who unavoidably has encounters with a variety of people representing the spectrum of natural—or unnatural—good looks. Ellie was right when she said that in order to be successful in the world of business, Zak would have to be somewhat immune to the allure of a pretty face or a perfect body. My logic seemed irrefutable. I had absolutely no reason to worry. The problem with cold, hard logic is that, no matter how solid it seems, it never really stands a chance against unbridled jealousy.

I tried to clear my head as I began my trek through the woods, but I found it hard to calm my wandering mind. I decided that focusing on Tanner's murder was the tamer of the subjects available to me, so I reviewed everything I currently knew.

Tanner had been a charter fishing captain on the lake since before I was born. He was a crusty old guy who admittedly was a bit rough around the edges, but he had a natural instinct that I would be willing to bet even the best equipment couldn't compete with. Tanner wasn't a rich man by any means, but his needs were simple, and he had a loyal following of hearty clients who returned for his wild tales, homemade moonshine, and natural knack for finding the best fishing spots year after year. The more I thought about it, the less inclined I was to believe that Gilbert French and his fancy new boat was as big a threat to Tanner as Levi believed.

A better question, I decided, was to ask myself whether Tanner was a threat to Gilbert. The transplant had obviously spent a lot of money on his fancy new boat. I had to wonder if his ability to steal customers from the old-school fishing charters on the lake was presenting a larger problem than he'd anticipated.

And then there were Tanner's other competitors. Tanner was known to be somewhat abrupt in his dealings with others as a general rule. Could the introduction of a new boat on the lake have created a tension that hadn't previously manifested itself as trickery and sabotage? I considered the charter companies I was familiar with and couldn't really identify a single prospective killer among the group. Still, it did seem like the natural balance they'd always enjoyed had been disrupted when the new guy arrived.

If Tanner's murderer hadn't been one of his competitors, then the next best guess was his ex-wife, Agatha. She had a reputation around town for being a witch. And I didn't mean a witch as in a bitch; I meant an honest-to-goodness, spell-casting witch. Most people realized that Agatha was living in an imaginary world most likely created by forty years of marriage to one of the orneriest men I've ever met. Still, there are those in town who believed her when she spouted off about her magical powers and potent spells.

I remembered hearing somewhere that Tanner was lobbying the state to have his ex-wife committed to a sanitarium. Personally, I think that might have been a bit over the top. Agatha had a vivid imagination and had been known to "curse" you if you angered her, but in spite of her little hobby, she seemed harmless enough. Besides, Tanner had been hit over the head with a cylindrical object, probably a bat, and not turned into a frog, so chances were the slightly mentally disturbed woman wasn't the slayer we were looking for.

If one of Tanner's competitors hadn't killed him, and Agatha hadn't killed him, who did that leave? A friend? A neighbor? An enemy of unknown origin?

I thought about Tanner's closest friends, most of whom attended the book club at the senior center where I volunteered. None seemed to have a mean bone in their bodies, so I moved on to his neighbors. Tanner lived in a small house near the marina where he kept his boat. Many of the homes in the area were owned by boat owners, while others had been turned into vacation rentals. I couldn't think offhand of anyone who would want to kill Tanner, but I didn't really know the man as well as some of the other members of the book club, so it made sense for me to call everyone together and ask them.

After returning to the boathouse, I showered and changed into jeans and a sweatshirt. I was about to head into town to run some errands when the phone rang. My heart skipped a beat as I prayed it was Zak and not some annoying telemarketer hoping to change my life with his newest product.

"Zak," I said, as I recognized the number on caller ID. "How's the trip?" I tried for a light tone I wasn't really feeling.

"Terrible."

I smiled.

"The plane was delayed in Chicago due to weather, and then, when we finally did take off, we were diverted through Phoenix."

"You went from Chicago to Phoenix on your way to New York?"

"We didn't get to the city until after midnight. I wanted to call but hated to wake you."

"That's okay. I probably left my phone off anyway. You know me, Miss Absentminded."

Zak laughed. "I'm glad you weren't worried."

"Why would I worry?" I was trying to sound like I didn't have a care in the world. "Besides, if I were going to worry, I'd be worried about Tanner Brown's murder and its effect on Hometown Christmas."

"Tanner Brown was murdered?"

I spent the next twenty minutes filling Zak in on the developments of the past twenty-four hours, including Tanner's murder and our current list of suspects, the county's challenge to the operating permit for the Zoo, and Earl Fielder's auto accident, which had turned out to be much more serious than we originally realized. Zak offered his input on the murder investigation, promised to look into the permit, and said he'd call me later that evening. By the time I hung up, I felt better than I had since he'd left.

Chapter 11

"Did you hear about Tanner Brown?" I asked Jeremy, who was working on the new cages we were building when I arrived at the shelter.

"Yeah. Everyone is talking about it. Any idea who did it?"

"Not a clue. The gang and I are working on it."

"Figured you would be. Heard they closed the community center. They plan to move Santa's Village to the gym at the high school. What are we going to do?"

"Solve a murder."

"I figured you'd say that, too. I was thinking about possible suspects and wondered if anyone had picked up Buddy," Jeremy said.

Buddy! How could I have forgotten about Tanner's golden retriever?

"I'll head over there now," I decided. "I'll leave Lambda here with you but take Charlie. If the poor dog has been left alone, he might be a bit skittish."

"Okay. Let me know if you need me to do anything," Jeremy offered.

******

During the forty years or so that Tanner had owned the little house near the marina, the area had changed from a downtrodden fishing village to an upscale resort dominated by high-dollar vacation rentals. I knew that several of Tanner's neighbors had complained about his failure to keep up exterior maintenance over the years, but until I pulled up in front of the dilapidated house sandwiched between two lakefront estates, I hadn't realized how much the marina had really changed.

I knocked on the door in case Agatha had returned to the two-bedroom cottage. When she didn't answer, I let myself in. Buddy was nowhere in sight, but there was a note on the kitchen table, letting whomever might come looking that the next-door neighbor on the right had taken the dog to her place after she'd learned of Tanner's death. I decided to check out the situation, so I left and walked down the beach to the neighboring house.

"Morning," I greeted the woman, who was shoveling the snow from her deck. "My name is Zoe Donovan. I came by to check on Buddy and saw your note."

"You're the one who works at the shelter." The woman looked to be in her midfifties, with thick brown hair peppered with gray twisted into a braid that trailed down her back.

"I did."

"I heard the shelter closed down and didn't know who to call, so I brought Buddy over here when I heard about Tanner. It's such a shame."

"It really is," I agreed.

"Come on in. I could use a break anyway. We'll have a cup of coffee and chat about what to do about Buddy. He's such a sweet old dog."

I was willing to bet that Buddy had already found a home with a woman who seemed to care about him.

Unlike Tanner's little shack, the woman, who introduced herself as Polly, lived in a large three-story structure that had to contain at least five thousand square feet of beautiful living space. Polly indicated that I should take a seat at the little breakfast table tucked inside a nook overlooking the lake while she made the coffee.

"Your home is beautiful," I commented.

"Thanks. I like it."

"I had no idea the area had changed so much over the past few years. Last time I was over this way, the houses all looked more like Tanner's."

I could hear a dog barking and kids laughing in the background. I imagined that Buddy was playing with the woman's kids or grandkids.

"Four years ago Edward Harrington built that huge house on the west edge of the village," Polly explained. "Once that house went in, the perceived value of the surrounding property rose exponentially. Within the next two years, most of the previous residents sold their property for a huge profit. The little old homes were torn down, and the new, bigger ones were built in their place. Tanner was the last holdout. I can't tell you how many people have tried to buy his property, but he steadfastly refused to sell."

"I guess that didn't go over too well with his neighbors."

"Not at all. Several of the people in the area, including Gary Conway, his neighbor on the other side, complained to the town about Tanner's eyesore. Most hoped the city would force him to sell, or at least modernize his property, but the town attorney determined that having a small house—even a small, run-down house—wasn't against the law. Their hands were tied."

Sounded like a motive for murder to me.

"I know this is none of my business," I began, "but can you give me an idea what Tanner's property would likely go for?"

"Couple million, at least."

A couple million? That sounded like another motive for murder. I assumed that ex-wife Agatha was now the sole owner of the property, able to sell if she chose.

"Wow. I can't believe Tanner held out for so long. He could have retired."

"I think that was his plan," Polly said. "He mentioned that he planned to sell his boat as well as his house and move to Arizona."

So much for motives. If he planned to sell the house and his neighbors knew that, then why kill him? All they'd needed to do was wait. And Agatha? Sure, two-million dollars was better than one, but was double the money worth the risk? Knowing Agatha, I doubted it.

I really hate it when I think I'm getting somewhere but then quickly discover I'm not.

"So about Buddy . . ." I began. "I'm happy to take him, if need be, but I'm sure he'd rather stay here with you and your kids until all the details are worked out."

"Grandkids," Polly corrected. "And I'd be happy to keep him. Buddy and I have forged a relationship of sorts since I've lived here. I already spoke to Penelope, but she wants nothing to do with the dog."

I wasn't surprised to hear that Penelope didn't want Buddy, because Kendra had complained to me on more than one occasion that her mother wouldn't let her have animals when she was growing up, which was most likely why she was afraid of them now.

"So unless Agatha wants him," Polly continued, "consider my home to be his new home."

"Fantastic," I said. "I'll see if I can track down Agatha and let you know what she wants to do. I've known her for a long time, and she's never really liked the dog. She's definitely more of a cat person."

"You mean a black-cat person," Polly teased.

"I guess you've heard about her little hobby."

"I have. It's fascinating, really. Still, I agree that Buddy will be better off with me."

Chapter 12

After I left the marina, I decided to stop by the high school and check on Santa's Village. Sheriff Salinger wouldn't let anyone inside the community center, so the extensive backdrop that made the Village so magical was missing, but someone had set up a chair and ropes for the line. I saw that Pappy was in attendance as the jolly old man himself.

"Have you heard from Earl?" I asked Hazel, who was managing the long line of sugared-up kids.

"He's still in the hospital. I heard he's expected to be in there a few more days at least."

"Was he seriously injured?"

"A broken leg, a sprained wrist, a slight concussion, and a load of cuts and bruises. The biggest problem is his inability to get around on his own."

"Charlie and I will stop in and check on him later." I looked across the room to where Charlie was entertaining a group of children. "It seems like

Santa's Village is doing well in spite of the last-minute change in venue."

"It's such a shame we weren't able to move the Village." The mechanical elves, bucking reindeer, and forest animals took days to set up. Even if Salinger did let a crew in to retrieve the props, it wouldn't be feasible to move everything. "The kids don't seem to mind, but a lot of the adults have commented that the Village just isn't the same without them."

"I have to admit I'm a little worried about the pet adoption."

"Surely the sheriff will open the center by Wednesday?"

"I hope so, but you never know what Salinger will do." I waved at Willa Walton, who was handing out candy canes. "Maybe the weather will hold and I can find an outdoor venue."

"I heard there was a forty-percent chance of snow next weekend," Hazel pointed out.

"Yeah, but that translates to a sixty-percent chance of no snow. I prefer to remain optimistic at this point." I smiled as one of the kids put a Santa hat on Charlie, who very patiently posed for a photo.

"I've noticed your ads around town. You've managed to generate quite a bit of interest. It was a good idea to include the photos of some of the pets that will face death if not adopted."

"Some of the other shelters in the county have called in the past few days. We're up to forty dogs and thirteen cats."

"That's a lot even for you," Hazel pointed out.

"I know, but I have a good feeling about the weekend. There's this holiday energy in the air. Now all I have to do is solve a murder and we'll be set."

"Maybe you could use one of the other classrooms in the school."

"I've already asked him, and Principal Lamebrain said no. In fact, he's trying to figure out a way to revoke the permit I already have for the gym. He says that I didn't disclose that the facility would be used to house animals at the time I applied to use it."

"Do you think he'll pull the permit?" Hazel wondered.

"No. It'd be bad publicity for the school. There are fliers in every business with a bulletin board within sixty miles, and ads in every paper. It'd look bad if he canceled the event for no good reason."

"Zoe." My dad walked up and kissed me on the cheek as Hazel excused herself. "I'd like you to meet Blythe Ravenwood. She just recently moved to Ashton Falls."

"Glad to meet you." I smiled suspiciously at the woman, who looked a bit more chummy with my father than I was comfortable with.

"Blythe is a retired schoolteacher," my dad informed me. "She bought the old Thompson place."

"Your father has been such a gem, helping me with the remodel," Blythe said.

"You've been helping?" I was surprised he hadn't mentioned his new lady friend before today.

"Blythe came into the store a month or so ago looking for supplies. I offered to help her with a few projects. The house is coming along real nice."

"You'll have to come to Sunday dinner so I can show you what we've done," Blythe invited. "Perhaps this weekend?"

"I appreciate the invitation, but I'm pretty busy for the next few weeks. Maybe after the New Year."

"Of course, dear. I forget how busy you youngsters are likely to get."

I tried not to take offense at the *dear* and *youngsters*, but I was pretty sure I hated my dad's new friend already. Keep in mind that I prefer a predictable equilibrium in my most important relationships, and the fact that my dad had a new friend he hadn't mentioned to me wasn't sitting well at all.

"Your dad told me you recently lost your job."

"Yeah, the county closed the shelter, but I'm working to reopen it as a private enterprise," I answered Blythe's inquiry.

"Really? Where did you get your business degree?"

"I don't have a degree, but I know what I'm doing," I assured the pushy woman.

"I'm sure you do, dear."

"Zoe is extremely organized and very smart," my dad assured his friend. "In fact, she's serving as the chairperson for this year's Hometown Christmas."

"Quite an honor for such a young woman."

"I'm twenty-four," I pointed out.

"I apologize. I thought you were younger. Perhaps it's the hair. I can recommend a good hairdresser in Bryton Lake. A professional image is so important nowadays."

"Thanks, but I have my own hairdresser." The fact of the matter is, due to my petite size and slight frame, I'm often mistaken for a fourteen-year-old. Most times I don't mind the assumption, but Daddy's new friend was most definitely rubbing me the wrong way. I know; I promised to try to be more open-minded about the leeches who attach themselves to my people. And I'd made great progress with Barbie, Levi's yoga-instructor girlfriend. But my dad? That was another matter altogether.

"Blythe and I were just heading out to do some shopping, but I saw you talking to Hazel and wanted to introduce you."

"It was nice to meet you," I said politely. "Have a nice time shopping. And Dad," I added, "call me later. It's important."

"I will." My dad kissed me on the cheek again and then ushered Blythe toward the door.

******

After leaving Santa's Village, I called Levi and Ellie and asked if they wanted to come over for a strategy session that evening. They both agreed and were pulling up just as I arrived home. Ellie had volunteered to bring something to make for dinner, so Levi suggested that he take the dogs out for a run on the beach while Ellie and I prepared what she'd brought.

"Have you met my dad's new girlfriend?" I asked as we began gathering supplies for the casserole we were making.

"Your dad has a girlfriend?"

"Her name is Blythe Ravenwood. Apparently, she's just moved to town. I'm pretty sure she's evil."

"Evil?" Ellie laughed as she began browning ground beef in a frying pan.

"She called me *dear* and said I looked younger than twenty-four."

"*Dear* is a term of endearment, and we both know you *do* look younger than twenty-four."

"She has a wide streak of gray in otherwise black hair," I said as I handed Ellie the sour cream. "I'm pretty sure that's a witch thing."

Ellie rolled her eyes. "I thought you were going to try to work on this irrational jealousy you have toward everyone who tries to penetrate your inner circle."

"I know." I sighed. "It's just that my dad has known her a *month* and he's just now mentioning her?"

"I'm sure there's nothing serious going on between them. If there was, he would have told you."

"Yeah, I guess," I begrudgingly agreed.

"As soon as you finish slicing the mushrooms, go ahead and start the water for the noodles."

Ellie was making her easy ground beef stroganoff, which smelled heavenly.

"Levi mentioned that you were going to get a tree for Santa's Village tomorrow," Ellie said as she stirred the sour cream into the beef-and-mushroom mixture.

"Yeah. I'm afraid Santa's Village needs all the help it can get, and I figured it would be nice to have one for the pet adoption as well. Want to come?"

"I wish I could, but I have to work. Whatever you do, don't let Levi pick the tree. He always cuts the one closest to the road for his own place. A nice big tree with full branches will put everyone in the Christmas spirit."

"Don't worry. I'll make sure we get a big one. Can you hand me that olive oil?" I asked as I prepared a salad to go with the casserole.

"Of course, we still need to solve Tanner's murder. Any luck with the investigation?" Ellie asked as she gave me the bottle.

"I went by Tanner's house today," I informed her. "I wanted to check on Buddy but ended up having a nice conversation with a neighbor. Have you been over to the marina lately?"

"Not for a few years. I hear it's changed."

"Like how." I described the new homes and upscale atmosphere, and filled Ellie in on Tanner's refusal to sell until recently, and his neighbors' distress over living next to what amounted to less than a shack in comparison to their homes. As I had, Ellie speculated over whether his refusal to sell could have been a motive for murder, but I argued that the timing seemed off because he'd recently changed his mind.

"Yeah, but what if the killer didn't know he'd changed his mind?" Ellie asked. "It seems like his decision to cash in and move was pretty recent."

I hadn't thought of that, but she was right. Maybe one of his uppity neighbors had killed him in order to remove the eyesore they thought they were stuck with.

"It seems like we have a lot of different motives, but I don't see how we're going to narrow it down." I sighed.

"You can eliminate Agatha. Mom said she moved to Salem, Massachusetts, a month ago. She was on a pilgrimage to find the roots of her witchy heritage."

"Okay, so that leaves us with his competitors and his neighbors," I summarized.

"Whoever killed Tanner was most likely seen at the community center by someone the night he was killed. The room where Tanner died is in the back of the building, but the back door was locked. Someone had to have come in through the front door. We can make a list of neighbors and competitors and ask Hazel who was there."

"Good idea." Hazel had been monitoring the door most of the evening. "I wonder what, if anything, Salinger has uncovered."

"If you talk to Zak, you should ask him to snoop around to see what he can find out," Ellie suggested. "He did help you out by hacking into the coroner's records when you were investigating the turkey farm murder last month. I'd be willing to bet he can get into Salinger's files as well."

"Let's just hope he doesn't end up in jail."

"Who's in jail?" Levi walked in through the back door with the dogs.

"No one yet. We were thinking of asking Zak to hack into Salinger's files," I explained.

"Zak knows what he's doing. I wouldn't worry about it," Levi assured me. "If we're talking murder, I found out some info on the fishing-boat controversy. It seems that Gilbert French wasn't raking in the bucks with his high-tech fishing charters like you might think. In fact, the exact opposite was pretty much occurring. Most of the men and women who come to the lake to fish do so because of the laid-back atmosphere. Based on what I've been told, Gilbert was seriously thinking about folding up his boat and moving to a bigger lake. One of the guys at the high school told me that Gilbert had already spoken with a commercial fishing enterprise on Lake Superior."

"So Gilbert would have no motive to kill Tanner," I realized. "What about some other competitor?"

"My contact seemed to think that with Gilbert leaving the scene, the equilibrium that had always existed among the charter boats would be restored."

"I thought someone sabotaged Tanner's boat," I pointed out. "Wasn't that the reason he was moving in the first place?"

"Word around the lake is that it was Agatha who was behind the problem with the boat. She'd wanted to cash out and leave the area for quite some time. Apparently, Tanner gave her some money for a trip with the promise to tie things up while she was gone. As strange as this sounds, it seems like Tanner and Agatha were getting along better than ever once she left and he agreed to move on."

"So that leaves us with a disgruntled neighbor who may not have known that Tanner finally decided to sell," Ellie said.

"Ken Barnett told me that Tanner listed the house with him two weeks ago. Ken attended the last homeowners' meeting and asked for cooperation during the sale," Levi informed us.

"There's a homeowners' association?" I asked. "In Ashton Falls?"

"I guess after new people moved here and built those million-dollar houses, they wanted to protect their investment and formed their own association."

"So if Tanner's competitors don't have a motive and his neighbors don't have a motive and Agatha is on the East Coast, we're back to square one," I summarized.

"Looks like it," Levi stated the obvious.

"Anyone have any other ideas?" I asked.

"What if Tanner wasn't the victim?" Ellie hypothesized.

"Come again?" I asked.

"What if the killer was a Santa hater who would have killed anyone in the outfit?"

"Or," I suggested excitedly, "what if the intended victim was Earl Fielder and not Tanner Brown? Earl was supposed to play Santa last night and everyone in town knew it. Only a few of us were aware of the switch. The killer must have been waiting in the room we used for Santa to change. It could have been dark when Tanner first walked in there."

"Okay," Ellie said, "then who would want to kill Earl?"

Chapter 13

The next morning, Levi, Charlie, Lambda, and I went deep into the forest in search of the perfect tree. I was sorry Zak couldn't have been there. He would have enjoyed the trek on snowshoes into a part of the forest tourists from off the mountain didn't know about. It was a beautiful, sunny day, and the sky was about as blue as I'd ever seen it. I know Ellie was disappointed that she wasn't able to go with us, but I was glad to have some time alone with Levi. It had been quite a while since we'd really talked.

"This has to be the most perfect day we've had in a long time," I commented as we trudged through the snow-covered evergreens, pulling a sled behind us. The dogs had taken to walking behind the sled in order to take advantage of the trail Levi and I had forged.

"It really is." Levi turned his head slightly so I could hear him from his position slightly in front of me. "I tried to get Barbie to go cross-country skiing with me, but she was having none of it."

"She more of a downhill girl?"

"She's more of a nothing-that-requires-trudging-through-snow girl."

"Do the two of you have plans for Christmas?" I wondered.

"I don't know. Maybe. She wants to go to New York for a couple of weeks while I'm on winter break. I'm considering it, but I still haven't made up my mind."

"Winter break starts in three days," I pointed out. "I would think you'd have needed to purchase airline tickets before now."

"Barbie has tickets. She's leaving on the twentieth with or without me and staying through New Year's. The thought of being away from everyone for both Christmas and New Year's doesn't quite sit right, but she is my girlfriend, and she does have a point that it's not like I have family in the area."

"That's true." What I really wanted to do was remind him that Ellie and I were his family, but I was sure he knew that in spite of what he'd just said.

"My sister lives a few hours away from where Barbie's parents live, and it would be nice to visit with her for a few days. I know we haven't always gotten along, and her husband is a putz I can barely stand to be in the same room with, but I guess family is family."

I paused to adjust the strap on my snowshoe. "It would be nice to visit your sister," I agreed. "Still, Ellie and I will miss you if you aren't around for our annual Christmas Eve dinner and gift exchange."

"Yeah, I thought of that."

I felt bad for Levi. I had my dad and Pappy, and Ellie had her mom, but Levi had no one in the area.

The three of us have traditionally gotten together every Christmas Eve, but most years I have dinner with Dad and Pappy, and Ellie spends time with her mom on Christmas Day. Levi claims he's happy for the solitude, but I was willing to bet that solitude on Christmas wasn't really all it was cracked up to be.

Levi paused to look around, and I made my way forward until I stood next to him. I put my arm around him and leaned my head against his shoulder. "I think you should go."

"You do?"

"Yeah. You should spend time with your sister and her family. You have a brand-new nephew you've barely even met. You and Ellie and me can have our dinner and gift exchange after you get back."

"I suppose I could just go for part of the time. The tickets Barbie bought have us leaving on the twentieth and returning on January third. Two weeks seems long."

"It'll be hard to change the tickets during the holiday rush," I pointed out. "Two weeks will fly by. You can spend some of your time with Barbie and some of your time with your sister. You could even pop down and see your mom." Levi's mom had moved to Florida a while back, and he had yet to visit her there.

Levi put his arms around me and hugged me, resting his chin on the top of my head as he considered the idea. I leaned into the man I considered one of my best friends and realized that with everything that had happened of late, we really hadn't had time to share the easy silences that we'd always had between us. I listened to his heart beat as the minutes ticked away. I would miss Levi if he decided to go, but deep down I knew it was time for him to make peace with his family.

"So are things serious with Barbie?" I found myself asking.

Levi took a step back. "Not really. I don't know. Maybe."

"That sounds definitive." I laughed.

"Barbie seems to want to move things to the next level. She's mentioned our moving in together. But I don't know." Levi frowned. "I like Barbie and we have fun together, but moving in . . . that's a step I'm not sure I'm ready to take with anyone."

"So don't move in. You're twenty-four years old. You have plenty of time to figure out who you want to spend your life with," I advised.

"That's what I told her, but Barbie can be very persuasive."

"Yeah, I'll bet," I teased. If there's one thing you can say for Barbie, she is drop-dead gorgeous, and she knows how to use her long blonde hair, deep blue eyes, and hourglass figure to capture and hold the attention of anyone with a Y chromosome. "Just remember that Barbie can be persuasive with men in general. I don't want to see you get hurt."

"I know." Levi started walking down the hill we were standing on. "I don't want to see me get hurt either. The thing is, I don't think I'd be hurt if Barbie decided to *be persuasive* with another man. I guess that bothers me more than I like."

"You figure you must not love her if you're not jealous of her attentions to other men?"

"Something like that."

"And you think you might be sending the wrong message if you went to New York with her for Christmas."

"Exactly."

"So don't go."

"I thought you said I should."

I had to admit Levi's Christmas dilemma was a bit more complicated than I'd originally realized.

"How about you? Any special plans for Christmas?" Levi asked when I didn't respond.

I shrugged. "I guess I'll spend the day with my dad and Pappy, like always. I'm sure Ellie and I will hang out at some point as well."

"And Zak?"

I thought about my gorgeous neighbor and his equally gorgeous houseguest. "I don't know. He asked me to the ball, so I'll see him then. We really haven't discussed anything beyond that. His business partner has been staying with him, so he might have plans."

"I've seen his business partner." Levi grinned. "Now there's a woman who can distract a man."

Terrific.

"I think I see the perfect tree," Levi said, thankfully changing the subject. "That tall one at the bottom of the hill."

"That tree is like thirty feet tall. We'll never get it back to the truck," I pointed out.

"Not that one; the one to the right of it."

I looked to where Levi was pointing. There was a tree about twelve feet tall, with a nice shape and thick branches. "It's perfect."

"Good thing we brought the sled. It'd be heavy to carry all the way back to the truck."

"Yeah, good thing."

I waited as Levi continued down the hill in front of me with the sled behind him and the dogs behind me. I was glad I'd thought to wear my long johns under my ski pants. In spite of the sunny sky, the temperature was lingering around twenty degrees. The trek through the snow was keeping me warm, but I knew that once I stopped walking the cold would set in.

"The more I think about it, the more I like the idea of the trip." Levi set down his backpack next to the tree we'd identified and took out his saw. "But I feel a little weird about leaving you and Ellie when there's a killer on the loose."

"You aren't leaving until the twentieth, and we'll have the murder investigation all wrapped up by the eighteenth at the latest."

"How do you know that?"

"Because it has to be. The lives of more than fifty animals depend on it. Trust me when I tell you that we're going to solve this puppy in the next few days."

"You know, I bet you'll do just that. I've got all day. How can I help after we deliver the tree?"

"I've been thinking about the idea that Earl could have been the intended victim. He's been acting oddly lately. It might be worth our while to have a chat with his wife, and Betty always has had an appreciation for the male gender."

"You want me to flirt with her?"

"Just a little."

"She's like sixty."

"It's for a good cause."

"Oh, very well."

Chapter 14

After we dropped off the tree at the gym, I left Lambda at the boathouse before Charlie and I headed to the hospital. Levi had agreed to stop by to talk to Betty while Charlie and I found out what we could from Earl.

The Ashton Falls Community Hospital is a small facility with basic services and a local clientele. Patients with serious injuries or life-threatening diseases are transported to the larger hospital in Bryton Lake.

I stopped into the gift shop next to the hospital and purchased a cheerful floral arrangement with a Christmas theme before heading to Earl's room.

"Zoe," Earl said as I entered his room and set the red and white flowers arranged with evergreen branches on his bedside table. "What a beautiful bouquet. It's so Christmassy."

"I thought you might need some cheering up." I took the chair next to the bed while Charlie sat patiently on the floor next to me. "How are you feeling today?"

"Like I smashed my car into a tree."

I smiled at Earl's honesty. "Hazel said you're going to be laid up for a while. I know you must be disappointed to miss the Christmas season."

He shrugged.

Since Earl was normally Mr. Christmas 365 days a year, I found it odd that he seemed so apathetic about the necessity of sitting out what has historically been his favorite time of the year.

"So what happened?" I asked.

"Someone—probably a tourist without snow tires—swerved in front of me. I managed to avoid a head-on collision by running my car into a ditch."

"And the other driver?" I asked.

"Didn't even stop. If you ask me, I think she was drunk."

"Has the sheriff arrested her?"

"I'm afraid I didn't get a good look. All I remember is that the car that almost hit me was a late-model Ford sedan. Dark blue or black," he added.

"But you're sure it was a woman driving?"

"Actually, I'm not. I didn't see the driver's face, but I did notice that the driver had on one of those knitted hats. A red one. Didn't figure a man would wear something like that."

"Do you think the accident was intentional?"

Earl looked shocked at the question. "Why would someone intentionally run me off the road?"

"I'm not saying anyone did. It was snowing and the roads were icy, and it most likely was nothing more than an accident."

"But?" Earl asked. "I can sense a *but* there."

I suppose I should have figured out how I was going to broach the situation with Tanner before I opened the door to this particular conversation. I wasn't even certain anyone had told Earl that Tanner was dead. But it was *the* topic of conversation in town, so I assumed someone had filled Earl in.

"I guess you heard about Tanner."

"I did. It's a damn shame. The guy was an ornery cuss, but I never really had a problem with him. Far as I know, he was a well-liked member of the community. Has the sheriff found out who's responsible?"

"Not yet."

"One of the nurses mentioned that he had a beef with some new charter company. It seems most of the folks around the hospital think he proved to be a threat to his new competition."

"Yeah, I heard that as well."

I sat quietly when a nurse came in to check the monitors. I needed to figure out a way to ease into the mistaken-identity theory without giving poor Earl a heart attack. His leg was in a cast and he had cuts on his hands and face, but he looked better than I imagined he might, considering the ordeal he'd been through. If our theory was correct, and someone was in fact trying to kill him, keeping the information from him didn't seem like the best course of action.

"I guess you heard that Tanner was filling in for you when he was killed." I had decided to jump in feet first after the nurse left the room.

Earl paled. A look of awareness crossed his face before he quickly turned away. If I hadn't been looking right at him, I might not have noticed his look of shock as he suddenly put two and two together. "No, I hadn't heard that," he eventually answered.

"What exactly have you heard?"

I could tell Earl was struggling to get his emotions under control before he spoke. "One of the nurses told me that Tanner had been found dead. Hit over the head. She really didn't elaborate, other than to speculate that it could have been business related."

I sat quietly and tried to figure out how to move the conversation forward.

"You think the killer meant the blow to the head for me?"

"The thought has crossed my mind," I admitted. "Tanner was a last-minute substitution, and he was killed after he returned to the room where he'd left his clothing. It was probably dark in the room, and he was wearing the Santa suit."

"Who would want to kill me?"

Poor Earl looked like he was going to be sick. Maybe this hadn't been the best idea. I certainly didn't want to make things worse for the guy.

"I was hoping *you* could tell *me*," I responded.

Earl's eyes grew big as, I imagine, he realized exactly who might want to kill him. "You're investigating?"

"I'm looking into it," I verified.

I waited while Earl struggled with an answer to the question I'd posed. I could tell he had a *someone* in mind, but for some reason he seemed reluctant to tell me who.

"And the sheriff?" Earl asked.

"He's probably looking into it as well."

"He hasn't been by," Earl said.

"I imagine he will be." Salinger was an idiot, but I was certain that even he would eventually put two and two together.

"I suppose you might want to talk to Gabe Turner," Earl provided.

"Gabe?"

"We had a bit of a falling out."

I frowned. Earl and Gabe had been friends for years. There was no way Gabe would hit Earl over the head as the result of a falling out.

"Can you tell me about it?"

"Betty and I are thinking about adding on a room," Earl started. "I went to talk to Gabe about some lumber, and he quoted me a price that was akin to highway robbery."

"And?" I prompted.

"And I told him as much. He got mad and slammed the door in my face. I haven't spoken to him since."

"I don't know," I responded. "Gabe has been known to have a temper, but he's not a killer. Are you sure his is the *only* name that comes to mind?"

Earl frowned.

"If my theory is correct, you could be in danger," I prompted. "We really should fill the sheriff in on this line of reasoning."

"No!" Earl shouted. "Don't involve the sheriff. At least not yet. Not until we're certain."

"Are you sure?" I asked.

"I'm sure. Promise me."

I hesitated.

"I'll tell you what I know, but you have to promise that we'll keep this between ourselves."

"Levi is helping me. Ellie, too."

"Okay, you can share what I'm about to tell you with them, but no one else. You have to promise me."

I wasn't sure I was comfortable with making such a promise, but I realized Earl wasn't going to tell me anything unless I agreed to his terms.

"Okay, I promise. But only until we know for sure. If we find the killer, I have to tell Salinger everything."

I noticed that Earl was sweating, although the temperature in the room was pleasant. He wiped his forehead as he began his incredible story.

******

"Are you sure he wasn't pulling your leg?" Levi asked two hours later, as we headed toward Bryton Lake.

"Why would he do that?"

"I have no idea, but the story seems a bit far-fetched."

Levi was right. It *was* far-fetched, but it was the only lead we had, and I couldn't imagine why Earl would lie to me.

Apparently, his Secret Santa gift this year involved the gas station at the edge of Ashton Falls. The owner, Garver Arnold, had decided to retire after more than forty years manning the pumps and was putting the facility up for sale. His longtime employee, Brian Kitterman, had expressed the desire to buy the gas station but was unable to put together enough cash for a down payment.

While Brian was working to procure the needed funds, Roy Burgis, a gas station owner from Bryton Lake, had put in an offer on the business. When Earl found out, he appealed to Garver's sense of community and asked him to give Brian a bit more time to work things out. According to Earl, Garver was reluctant but agreed after Earl promised to help Brian come up with the down payment. According to Earl, Roy was furious that he'd gotten involved and messed up what he considered to be a sweet deal. Earl claimed he'd received threatening letters from Roy, telling him to butt out of matters that were none of his concern.

"I can see why this Roy Burgis might be ticked off," Levi commented as we slowly made our way down the narrow mountain road connecting Ashton Falls to the valley below, "but I don't see how messing up a business deal would be a motive for murder."

"Yeah." I glanced out of the window as the snow turned to sleet. "The whole thing seems odd to me, too, but Earl seemed adamant that Roy was our guy. I figured it wouldn't hurt to check him out."

"What time is Ellie coming over with dinner?" Levi asked.

"Around six." When I'd called Ellie and told her that I'd have to cancel the plans I'd made with her for the afternoon, she'd volunteered to bring dinner to the boathouse.

"It's going to be tight if this snow doesn't let up."

"I'll give her a call and tell her to plan on us being there closer to seven."

I took my cell phone out of my pocket and turned it on. "Damn."

"Do you always swear at your phone?" Levi wondered.

"Two missed calls, both from the same number."

I felt the color leave my face as I listened to the first message. There are times when I'm convinced that I'm cursed, and that the powers that be might be taking great delight in messing with my sanity.

"Problem?" Levi asked.

"Dusty's Delights is going out of business."

"And this Dusty is a friend of yours?" Levi was clearly confused by my distress.

"Dusty is the main food vendor for Hometown Christmas. He left a message saying he's packing up his spatula and moving to Maui, effective immediately."

"You have more than one food vendor," Levi pointed out.

"Yeah, folks selling cider, fudge, and candy apples. Dusty was scheduled to operate the main kitchen. He planned to set up booths in the gym, offering a variety of menu options, including several different types of soup served in bread bowls, pulled pork and shredded beef sandwiches, bratwurst, and corn dogs. You know, standard festival food. If I can't find a replacement in the next three days, our food court will be more of a snack line guaranteed to provide a sugar high but little else."

"Doesn't this Dusty have a contract?"

"He does, although I don't suppose I have a lot of recourse against a business that has gone under. What am I going to do?"

Levi wove the fingers of his right hand through my left hand and squeezed my hand in support. "Don't worry. We'll figure something out. We're just about to the intersection Earl mentioned. Keep your eye out for the address he gave you."

I looked down at the paper in my hand and studied the directions. "It must be that place on the corner."

"Wow."

"Yeah, wow," I agreed. The gas station Roy Burgis owned was the Cadillac of gas stations. Not only did it have twelve rows of pumps—six with unleaded and six with diesel—but the attached restaurant and mini-mart was larger than the market in Ashton Falls. As we pulled in and found a parking spot, I had to wonder why someone who owned a gas station as nice as the one we were sitting in front of would even want the two-pump station on the mountain.

"Are you sure this is the right place?" Levi asked.

"It's the address Earl gave me."

"Why would someone who owns this even want Garver's old station?"

"My thought exactly."

"Do you think we've been had?"

"I think maybe we have."

******

A brief discussion with Mr. Burgis confirmed what Levi and I already suspected. Earl, for reasons I still hadn't figured out, had vastly exaggerated Roy's interest in Garver's gas station. Yes, he'd put in an offer, but he claimed his interest was mostly just a whim, and when Garver refused to sell the station to him, he'd moved on to other things. He adamantly denied sending threatening letters to Earl or anyone else.

"That was a huge waste of time," Levi commented as we started our drive back up the mountain.

"Why would Earl lie?"

"You said he was nervous about whatever he was hiding," Levi pointed out. "When I spoke to Betty, she appeared nervous as well. She didn't even invite me in. Maybe Earl sent us on a wild-goose chase to get us out of the way."

"Out of the way of what?"

"I have no idea."

"Something is definitely going on," I decided. "I think I'll pay another visit to Earl tomorrow. My instinct tells me he's in real trouble. He needs our help, whether he wants it or not."

"You can't save everyone," Levi said. "Especially someone who doesn't seem to want to be saved."

I knew Levi was right. Earl had intentionally led me down a rabbit hole. The question was, why?

Chapter 15

By the time we got back to the boathouse, I was exhausted. I'd called Ellie and explained the food-court situation, and she'd assured me she'd talk to her mom and, between them, they'd come up with a solution. If nothing else, she would run the kitchen with volunteers. Since the time period was so tight, we'd decided to skip dinner that evening so she could get started on the extensive amount of planning involved in providing the amount of food needed for the four-day event. And she'd told me that she'd made another batch of my grandmother's soup and left it in my refrigerator. She wanted me to taste it and call her that evening.

"What the . . ." I stopped on the threshold after opening the front door. "Marlow," I yelled.

It seemed that while Levi, Charlie, and I had been busy playing amateur detective, Marlow, my huge orange tabby, had been *un*decorating the twelve-foot tree Zak and I had put up over Thanksgiving weekend.

"Looks like someone was bored." Levi laughed at the strings of colored lights littering the floor.

"I'm going to kill that cat," I muttered under my breath as Lambda came trotting up to greet us with strands of tinsel hanging from his collar.

"Come on," Levi said as he removed the tinsel, "I'll help you clean up. We'll open a bottle of wine and order a pizza."

"Ellie left potato cheese soup," I informed Levi.

"Even better."

I stepped over a broken red globe as I entered the room. My black cat Spade was napping quietly on the back of the sofa, but Marlow was nowhere to be found. While both Marlow and Spade were rescues from the shelter I used to run, they were as different in personality as two cats could be. Spade—named after Detective Sam Spade and not the playing-card suit—was a petite black beauty, quiet and well-mannered from the day I brought him home, whereas Marlow—named after Detective Philip Marlowe—was a huge orange tabby with a mischievous streak and a playful manner.

Levi began gathering the strands of lights strung around the room while I made my way through the boathouse, turning on lights and searching for my naughty child. Most times, Marlow knew when he'd gotten himself into trouble, and he was probably hiding under the bed or in the closet.

"Come on out," I called. "I'm not really going to kill you, but I think we need to have a chat about the mess you made in the living room."

I climbed the stairs to my loft bedroom and looked under the bed. "I just bought a new bag of kitty treats," I said persuasively as I moved on to the closet. I searched in the bathroom, behind the shower curtain and under the sink. "This isn't funny anymore," I said, trying for a sterner voice. "I'm going to send Charlie after you if you don't show yourself right now."

"Meow." Marlow peeked out of the top of the clothes hamper. His green eyes seemed to beg for forgiveness, but I knew given the chance, he'd do the same thing all over again. I walked across the room and lifted him into my arms.

"I know you get bored when I'm gone all day, and I know those pretty little bird ornaments Ellie gave us have been driving you crazy since I hung them, but I really don't appreciate coming home to a mess."

Marlow began to purr. The silly cat hadn't understood a word I'd said. I settled the twenty-pound feline onto the bed while I changed into my comfy sweats and knee-high slippers.

I supposed the mess was partly my fault. I knew Marlow was fascinated by the bird ornaments, and I really shouldn't have tempted fate by hanging them near the top of the tree. I was thankful he hadn't gotten hurt. If I hadn't thought to secure the dang thing to the wall, the whole tree could have come tumbling down on top of him.

"Soup is heating," Levi called from downstairs. "What'd you do with your corkscrew?"

"Check the top drawer on the left side of the refrigerator," I called back.

"Red or white?"

"Red," I answered as I made my way back down the stairs.

"I see you found our feline felon."

Marlow was curled in my arms, content as a kitten who hadn't just destroyed the house. "Yes, we had a nice chat. He's sorry and promises never to do it again, but we might want to leave the birds Ellie gave me off the tree when we redecorate."

I set Marlow on the floor as I accepted the glass of wine Levi offered. He'd lit the fire and put on some Christmas music while I'd been upstairs. The lights I'd hung around the ceiling in my kitchen twinkled in the dim room.

"I've been thinking about our wild-goose chase," Levi said as he began rehanging the lights on the tree. "The more I think about it, the odder I find it that Earl lied to us. It's almost like he wanted to get us out of the way for the afternoon."

"Why would he want to do that?" I asked as I began sorting the red bulbs and other ornaments.

"I don't know," Levi admitted, "but something's going on. And I think there's more to it than just the murder. Earl has been acting strangely for a while now."

"According to the gossip gals," I said, referring to the women who manned the local gossip hotline, "Earl and Betty are having marital problems, which seems to fit with the fact that both Earl and Betty have been acting odd."

"Maybe, but I think there's more to it. When I talked to Betty today, she seemed scared. She didn't invite me in, and she kept looking over her shoulder, like she was expecting someone to come up behind her. I have classes tomorrow, but I think you should follow up with her in the morning. If Earl and Betty are in some kind of trouble, maybe we can help."

"I'll go first thing," I promised. "Do you want to get together after you get off work?"

"Barbie will be back tomorrow. We sort of made plans."

"Yeah, okay. I'll call you and fill you in on my talk with Betty. I plan to pay another visit to Earl as well. It looks like Tanner's murder might be connected to whatever it is they're hiding."

"As odd as it seems that they're hiding anything, I have to agree. Hey, this soup is really good," Levi added. "Is it your grandma's?"

"Ellie is trying to duplicate her recipe based on what we remember it tasting like. This batch is better than the last one, but I still think something is missing."

Levi took another sip. "I think your grandma's was creamier."

"Additional cream would make it thinner, and I don't think more cheese is the answer."

"Just tell Ellie creamier but not really cheesier. She'll figure it out. She's the best cook I've ever met."

"She certainly has a knack for it," I agreed.

"As long as Ellie is trying to duplicate your grandma's recipes, have her work on the fudge. I don't know what she did differently from everyone else, but your grandmother's fudge was the best I've ever tasted. I remember she made me a whole batch and wrapped it up in a Santa tin. I stuck it in the freezer and nibbled on it for months. Of course, I had to take it out of the tin and put it in a plain freezer container. I told my mom and sister that it was a science experiment for school so they wouldn't eat it."

"You're so mean. I'm sure there was enough to share."

"There are things you share and things you don't, and your grandma's fudge fell into the category of things you don't. I really miss your grandma. And not just because of the fudge."

"Yeah, me too. I thought I was having Ellie duplicate Grandma's recipe for Pappy, but I suddenly realized I was actually having her do it for myself. Christmas just hasn't been the same since she's been gone."

"Yeah, I know what you mean. Christmas has pretty much sucked since my dad died. And now that my mom and sister have moved away, the whole thing seems pretty pointless. Not that I don't love spending Christmas Eve with you and Ellie, but Christmas Day just seems like any other day. Maybe I will go to New York with Barbie. It'll be nice to change things up a bit."

Chapter 16

I got up early the next morning and headed over to Earl's place, only to find that Betty was gone. According to the next-door neighbor, Betty had decided to leave early for her sister's and wouldn't be back until after the New Year. As far as I knew, Earl was still in the hospital, so this turn of events made absolutely no sense at all. Why would Betty leave for the holiday early when her husband would be in no shape to travel for several more days at a minimum?

I headed over to the hospital. Earl was clearly hiding something, and I intended to find out what it was. I was more convinced than ever that Earl rather than Tanner was the intended victim of the Community-Center Killer, as folks in town were starting to refer to him or her. I hated to admit it, but it might be time to have a heart-to-heart with Salinger. Not that I relished the idea—and he'd probably tell me to butt out once he found out I was butting in—but Earl's life could be in real danger, and

I couldn't let my own selfish need to finish the job unaided get in the way of his safety.

"Morning Zoe," Dr. Ryder Westlake greeted me as I walked into the waiting area. "Where's Charlie?"

"At home babysitting Marlow."

"Come again?"

"Marlow, my orange tabby, is fascinated with my Christmas tree. He almost destroyed it while I was out yesterday, so I left Charlie home to keep an eye on it today."

"Keep an eye on it?"

"I explained to Charlie that Marlow wasn't allowed to play with the tree, and now every time Marlow even looks at it, Charlie chases him up the stairs."

Dr. Westlake laughed. "That's some dog you've got yourself."

"Yeah," I had to agree, "he really is. I'm here to see Earl, if he's available."

"I'm afraid they've taken him to X-ray. It could be an hour or more. You might want to come back after lunch."

I chatted with Dr. Westlake for a few more minutes. Not only is the man a babe, but he's kind and sweet and has an awesome sense of humor. When I first approached the hospital board about Charlie's dream of becoming a therapy dog, they'd been skeptical, but Dr. Westlake had stepped forward and spoken up on his behalf. Dr. Westlake was single, and on more than one occasion I'd considered taking him up on his standing invitation to dinner, but now, with Zak in the picture . . .

Actually, I'm not sure what, if anything, will come of my relationship with Zak, but I have to admit that there's a small part of me—okay, a huge part—that wants to find out.

"Are you going to the Holly Ball?" the doctor asked.

"I am."

"Save me a dance?"

"Count on it."

"Oh, by the way," Dr. Westlake stopped me as I turned to walk away, "During my rounds yesterday I overheard part of the conversation you were having with Earl about the series of events leading to Tanner Brown's murder. I thought you'd want to know that they've arrested the woman who ran Earl off the road."

The good doctor was correct; I *did* want to know. "Who was it?" I wondered.

"A woman by the name of Jennifer Haskell."

"Jennifer Haskell?" Jennifer Haskell was the mother of Toby Haskell, the ten-year-old boy who, as far as I knew, was still missing. "What happened?"

"I'm not sure. I overheard Sheriff Salinger telling Earl that she lost control of the car on the ice. It didn't seem like they were going to charge her with the accident, but there was talk of charges for leaving the scene of an accident."

"Did you happen to hear Salinger mention whether or not they'd found Toby?"

Westlake frowned. "Toby?"

"Her son Toby is missing." I realized that being relatively new in town, Dr. Westlake might not know much about the family. "He's run away before, more than once, so I think that's what the sheriff believes has occurred this time as well. I'm afraid his mom has a tendency to get hooked up with abusive men. Toby has been removed from the house on at least one occasion that I know of. I heard his mom got counseling, and I thought she was doing better, so I was surprised to hear he'd taken off again."

"I don't remember Salinger mentioning anything about Toby, but I was only there for part of the conversation."

"I guess I'll ask Earl. Thanks for the heads-up."

"Anytime."

******

I headed to Main Street from the hospital. I'd yet to do any Christmas shopping, and I only had nine days left. Normally, I bought gifts for my dad and Pappy, as well as Levi, Ellie, and Jeremy. This year I realized I'd need to add Zak to my list, and I had no idea what to get him.

As promised, he'd called every night after missing that first one. I'd lay in bed, curled up with my animals, wishing Zak was with me rather than thousands of miles away. Most nights we'd talk for hours, not about anything overly romantic but sharing how our day had gone and discussing things we'd like to do once he was able to stay in Ashton Falls for a while.

As I strolled through the festively decorated shops along the main drag, I tried to imagine what the perfect gift would be for a man who was just a friend on the surface, but really so much more.

Most years I got Levi a new sweater, sunglasses, or maybe some accessory for the many sports he played. Last year I got him new ski goggles, and the year before that, a regulator for his scuba gear.

Somehow, something awesome yet functional didn't seem quite right for Zak. I wanted to give him something personal without it being intimate. I was pretty sure we weren't up to intimate yet in our relationship.

"You look confused." Pappy walked up behind me as I stood staring at a table of men's cologne that Ernie had featured in the general store.

"Trying to decide what to get Zak for Christmas."

"Ah." Pappy smiled. "This must be the personal-but-not-intimate Christmas."

"You read my mind." I laughed. "I mean seriously, that's *exactly* what I was thinking. How did you do that?"

Pappy didn't answer, but he laughed back. *Rudolph the Red-Nosed Reindeer* came on over the loudspeaker in the much-too-crowded store. "I was thinking about taking a break from all this holiday hustle and grabbing a bite to eat. Care to join me?"

"I'd love to."

"Rosie's?"

"Sounds perfect. I need to ask Ellie about something and I know she's working today."

Pappy and I walked down Main Street hand in hand, stopping at each store to look at the windows. It was a cold day, with the high temperature reaching only into the twenties, but the air was calm and light snow lent a festive atmosphere to our small town. Main Street was busy as other last-minute shoppers bustled between the brightly lit shops.

"How's the investigation going?" Pappy asked.

"I'm not sure. I think Earl knows something he isn't admitting to. I stopped by the hospital, but he was in X-ray, so I'm going to head back over there after lunch. How's Santa's Village going?"

"I'm having the best time," Pappy admitted. "At first I wasn't thrilled about taking on the task, but I have to admit I haven't enjoyed the holiday as much since your grandma passed."

I hugged Pappy's arm. "I can't tell you how happy that makes me."

"I guess we're on for Christmas dinner?"

"We are," I confirmed. "I thought I'd invite Zak, if that's okay."

"Fine by me."

"I have a special dish I plan to make. It's going to be awesome, so come hungry."

"Always do."

"Levi decided to go to New York for Christmas, so I guess the Christmas Eve dinner Ellie, Levi, and I have won't happen this year. I should talk to Ellie about it. I'm thinking I'll suggest the two of us do lunch instead of dinner this year."

Rosie's was packed with holiday shoppers, so Pappy and I headed back to the kitchen. Rosie kept a small table that sat four in a corner, to provide staff with a place to take a break away from the paying customers. Pappy and I sat down while Ellie dished out bowls of soup and sliced fresh-baked bread.

"I'm glad you stopped by." Ellie placed the food in front of us. "I was wondering if we could change our Christmas Eve dinner to a Christmas Eve lunch."

"I was just going to ask you the same thing. It works for me."

"Good." Ellie went back to assembling plates heaping with food for the patrons in the main dining room. "I may have plans that evening, but I wanted to be sure to make time for you as well."

"You have plans as in a date?" I found myself asking.

"I don't know if you'd call it a date, but I may be having dinner with a friend I'd prefer not to discuss just yet."

"Oh, a mystery lover. I like a good mystery," I teased.

"He's not my lover," Ellie said, defending herself.

"So when do I get to meet this *not a lover*?"

"Soon." Ellie blushed.

******

After Pappy and I finished our lunch, he went on with his shopping and I returned to the hospital. Luckily, Earl was back from X-ray and resting comfortably in his room.

"Zoe, I didn't expect to see you here today." Earl forced a smile, but I could tell he was less than enthusiastic about my unannounced visit.

"I checked out the lead you gave me yesterday."

He actually blushed.

"It seems you may have exaggerated Roy Burgis's interest in Garver's property."

"I'm sorry you wasted your time." Earl seemed genuinely regretful, so why the subterfuge?

"I heard they found the woman who ran you off the road."

"It appears so."

"Dr. Westlake told me they think it was an accident."

"That's what Salinger said. Icy roads and all."

"And I understand Betty has left early for her sister's."

"Yeah." Earl was beginning to sweat. "No use her sitting around waiting on me."

"Cut the crap, Earl. What going on?"

He looked shocked that I'd been so blunt. Heck, *I* was shocked. In my own defense, I was tired, and Earl was clearly lying about pretty much everything. I had a Christmas fund-raiser and pet adoption to organize. The last thing I needed was someone sending me on pointless errands.

"If you don't tell me what you know, I'm going to go to Salinger and tell him everything I know." Which wasn't a whole lot, I had to admit.

"You can't do that." Earl looked seriously panicked. "Promise me you won't."

"Why shouldn't I? You're clearly hiding something. I'm trying to *help* you, but you have to tell me what's going on. What's *really* going on," I emphasized.

Earl looked around the room, as if afraid of being overheard. He lowered his voice. "If I tell you what I know, you have to promise to keep it to yourself."

"Tell me what you know and then I'll decide."

Earl shook his head. "No deal. Promise me or I won't talk."

It seemed I'd heard this speech before. "The truth this time?"

"The truth."

I sat down on the chair next to the bed. "Okay, spill."

"Two years ago, when I was volunteering at the library, I met a frightened young boy named Toby Haskell. He had a cast on his arm and a bruise on his eye, and after quite a lot of effort on my part, I got him to admit that his mother's boyfriend was beating him up."

Suddenly I knew exactly where this was going, but I let Earl finish.

"I reported the incident to Child Protective Services, and they promised to look into it. A case file was opened, and Toby's mom promised to stay away from the abusive boyfriend, and things seemed to get better for a while. Toby and I forged a relationship that has grown into a bond as strong as any I've ever known. Betty and I couldn't have children of our own, and I've spent my life working with other people's kids, enjoying every minute of it. But Toby is special. Toby feels like mine."

I sat quietly and waited while Earl gathered his thoughts.

"Early last summer, Toby showed up at my house with burn marks on his arm. He told me his mom's new boyfriend burned him with a cigarette when he accidently knocked over the man's beer. Once again I went to CPS, and they arrested the boyfriend and required the mom to get counseling. Toby was placed in foster care, which, by the way, he hated."

I bit my lip in order to fight back my tears as Earl continued.

"Two months ago, Toby was returned to his mother. At first things were great. He was *happy*. But in the past couple of weeks, I noticed a change in his behavior, though he insisted he was fine. Looking back on it, he clearly wasn't fine, but he was afraid of going back to foster care, so he kept his mouth shut when his mom's boyfriend took up where he left off after being released from jail after serving a ninety-day sentence."

"Poor Toby."

"Poor Toby is right. Two weeks ago, he came to me in the middle of the night. He'd been beaten badly. I wanted to take him to the hospital, but he refused. He told me he wasn't going back to foster care, and if I called the sheriff to report the incident, he'd run away and I'd never see him again. He's just a little boy."

Earl was weeping by this point.

"I didn't know what to do, so I took him in and promised I wouldn't tell anyone he was there. Betty and I decided to go visit her family for the holiday. We figured we'd use it as an excuse to sneak Toby away, and no one would ever know. We planned to make up some story about marital problems and eventually use that as an excuse to move ourselves."

"But his mom found out and ran you off the road."

"It looks like, although she hasn't said anything to Salinger about the possibility that I might have Toby, so I'm not certain what's going through her mind."

"Where is Toby now?"

"In Minnesota, with Betty. They left shortly after I sent you on your wild-goose chase."

"Why did you do it?"

"Because you're too perceptive for your own good. I was afraid you'd figure it out before I could get Betty and Toby on the road."

"Do you think Toby's mom killed Tanner, thinking it was you?" I asked.

"I don't know. Maybe."

I sat back in the chair and tried to figure out my next move. On one hand, if Toby's mom killed Tanner, she needed to be brought to justice, if for no other reason than she was obviously a danger to herself and others. On the other hand, if I told Salinger about Toby's mom's role in the murder, I'd have to reveal what I knew about Earl helping Toby. He could be charged with kidnapping. The fact that Betty had taken a ten-year-old boy across state lines without his parent's permission could even be a federal offense.

I didn't blame Earl and Betty for what they'd done. I'd probably have done the same thing. Earl had taken the legal route twice and had gotten little result. I knew in my heart that Toby was better off with Earl and Betty, and I certainly didn't want them to end up in prison for trying to help the boy.

Earl watched me as I tried to sort everything out in my head.

"I have to go."

"You won't tell," he insisted.

"I'll keep my promise."

Earl looked relieved.

"I'll come by to visit tomorrow. Get some rest."

As I made my way back to my truck, I tried to figure out my next move. How was I going to catch a killer without breaking my promise to Earl? The only thing to do, it seemed, was to pay a visit to the woman in question to see what she had to say for herself.

Chapter 17

Toby and his mom lived in a house in the shabby part of town. The front yard was littered with cigarette butts and beer cans, and there was a distinct smell of marijuana in the air. I carefully made my way across the rotted front porch and knocked on the door.

"I was wondering when you'd be by," Toby's mother said.

"You were?"

"Everyone in town knows that if there's a murder, you're right in the middle of it. Come on in." She opened the door and invited me into her worn but clean living room. "Can I get you some water?"

"No. I'm fine, thanks."

"Have a seat." She motioned toward the sofa.

"Are we alone?"

"We are," she confirmed.

I sat down on a sofa so tattered, a secondhand store would throw it away. The cushion had a huge dip in the center, causing me to sink into its softness.

As a result, my short legs didn't even reach the floor. Not exactly the position of power I was going for.

"I didn't kill that man." Jennifer jumped right in. "In fact, I was nowhere near the community center at the time of the murder."

"Can you tell me where you were?" I asked.

"Trying to save Earl."

"Trying to *save* Earl? By running him off the road?"

"Maybe it wasn't the best plan, but it was the only one I could come up with on short notice." Jennifer picked up a pack of cigarettes. "You mind?"

I did, but I said that I didn't. It was, after all, her home, so I supposed she could do as she pleased.

"My old man came home drunk, as usual. When he realized that Toby was gone, he put two and two together and figured that Toby would run to Earl. Earl has gone to the cops on two other occasions, and the last time it resulted in Drugger's incarceration. He said he was going to take care of things once and for all."

"So your boyfriend went to kill Earl?"

"It looked like. I freaked and called Earl's house. Betty said he'd already left for the community center. I needed to stop him without my old man realizing what I'd done. I figured if he was involved in a minor accident, he wouldn't show up to get himself killed, and Drugger would never know I'd intervened. I didn't mean for him to get hurt. If he'd ended up in the field, like I planned, he'd have been inconvenienced but fine. I didn't plan on him hitting a tree."

"So you stopped Earl, but Drugger didn't know it, so he went to the community center and killed Santa, who he thought was Earl?"

"It seems that way. I guess I didn't think it through. I just wanted to save Earl without getting myself involved. The guy's been real nice to Toby."

"Where is Drugger now?"

Jennifer shrugged. "Out. He comes and goes."

"You know that Betty has Toby?"

"Yeah, she called. I talked to him. He said he was happy. I ain't got no use for a kid. I told him he could stay."

That was something, but I wasn't sure it was enough to keep Earl and Betty out of prison if the entire truth came out. I needed to figure out a way to nail Drugger for Tanner's death without bringing the rest of the story into play. Maybe if I had the murder weapon or a bloody shirt, some piece of hard evidence that wouldn't require much of an explanation. Drugger might spill the beans about his suspicions regarding Toby, but he didn't have proof as far as I knew, and if I had Jennifer's cooperation, everything might just work out fine for everyone involved.

"Drugger. What's his real name?"

Jennifer blushed. "I honestly don't know."

******

"So how'd you convince Salinger that Drugger was his guy?" Zak asked later that night.

I was curled up in bed, with Charlie, Lambda, and the cats sleeping around me. It was snowing outside, and the flicker from the fire in the living room danced on the ceiling, exposed by the half wall separating the loft from the main part of the cabin. Soft music was playing on the stereo, giving the room a relaxing feel. It was a perfect romantic evening. Or at least it would have been, if Zak had been at the boathouse in person and not on the phone.

"It was easy. Drugger is an idiot. I found a bat with blood on it propped up against the bedroom wall. Add that to the fact that Salinger knows that Earl was responsible for sending Drugger to jail last summer and it was a slam dunk."

"And Toby?"

"He's with Betty. Jennifer told Salinger that Toby had run away but returned home, so she sent him to live with a relative out of state. The missing-persons report has been closed. I spoke to Earl, and he said he's going to pay to fly Jennifer to Minnesota for Christmas. Among the three of them, they're going to work it out, but it seems like Jennifer is willing to turn legal custody over to Earl and Betty."

"That's probably for the best."

"Yeah, it looks like things are working out for everyone. How's your software problem?"

"Almost fixed. I should be home late Wednesday night, if all goes as planned."

"Just in time for Hometown Christmas *and* the largest pet adoption event in county history. We're up to over a hundred animals."

"So the event is back on?"

"Yup. Salinger opened the community center, and Santa and his elves are moving back over starting tomorrow, leaving the gym free for the adoption event."

"That's fantastic news."

"And such a relief."

"I've missed you." Zak lowered his voice.

"I've missed you, too."

Chapter 18

"How'd the pet adoption go?" Ellie asked as I chopped greens to make a salad to go with the soup she'd brought. It was, she assured me, her third and final attempt to duplicate my grandmother's recipe.

"Fantastic," I answered as I picked up a piece of garlic bread off the cooling rack and took a bite. "We started the day with over a hundred animals and we're down to ten, which I'm confident we can place tomorrow."

"Wow. That's wonderful. When all those animals showed up this morning, I was sure I was going to have a houseful tonight." Ellie had volunteered to pet sit any animals that hadn't been adopted if I needed her to.

"Honestly, even I'm amazed we had so many people stop by. It helped that the adoption was held the same weekend as Hometown Christmas. We ended up with a lot of folks from off the mountain. If all goes well, we should have the remaining animals adopted by noon tomorrow."

"That's good because I was thinking about going shopping for a dress tomorrow afternoon, and I'd love for you to come with me."

"Dress?"

"For the ball. I'm thinking of driving down to the mall in Bryton Lake. I'd like to find something shocking."

"Shocking?" I laughed. Ellie was definitely not a shocking type of dresser. Levi *had* gone to New York with the *shockingly* beautiful Barbie, and I suspected Ellie was taking the whole thing a lot harder than she was letting on. "Do you have a date for the ball?"

Ellie nodded her head in the affirmative. "Rob asked me to go with him."

"Rob?" I questioned. "As in your ex-boyfriend Rick's brother Rob?"

"That's the one. He was in a bind a couple of weeks ago, and I volunteered to watch Hannah," Ellie said, referring to Rob's one-year-old daughter. "We've hung out a few times since then, and he invited me to attend the moonlight stroll and spend Christmas Eve with him and Hannah, since it would just be the two of them. He and Rick usually spend the day together, but Rick is going out of town this year, so Rob'll be on his own. And with Levi gone, I figured our plans might change as well." Ellie paused to take a breath. "Anyway, we got to talking about the fact that neither of us had a date for the ball, so we decided to go together. It's really just a friend thing, but I figured I might as well go all-out."

"Are you sure going out with Rob is a good idea?" I asked. "I mean, you just recently ended it with Rick."

"Rick is going to the dance with someone from work. And the two of us ended things as friends. He won't mind."

I hoped Ellie was right. The last thing we needed was a scene at the dance. Rob was a really great guy, and I could see how he and Ellie would be friends. He was Rick's older brother and so was a few years older than us. Like Gina, when his girlfriend had gotten pregnant, she'd made it clear she wasn't ready to be a mother, so Rob had taken on the responsibility and was raising Hannah on his own. He'd started the single parents group as a way for others in his situation to help each other out, and it seemed the group had developed into a supportive family.

I could see why Ellie would be attracted to a guy like Rob. She was the type of person who was born to be a mother. She'd spent many Friday and Saturday nights babysitting during junior high and high school, while Levi and I had been out tearing up the town.

"Besides," Ellie continued, when I didn't respond, "I've been thinking, and I've decided it's time to stop mourning things I'm never going to have and get on with my life. Going to the dance with Rob and spending Christmas Eve with him and Hannah will be good for me."

"You're talking about your feelings for Levi."

"Yeah, I guess it's been pretty obvious."

"Not obvious," I assured her. "But I am your best friend, and best friends know these things."

"Do you think Levi knows?" Ellie blushed.

I suspected he did but didn't want to ruin our relaxing evening. "He hasn't said as much." At least that was true; Levi had never come out and admitted that he knew Ellie had developed feelings for him.

"Good. I'd really rather he doesn't find out. He has Barbie now, and they seem really happy. I heard they were even talking about moving in together. I don't want to ruin our friendship by introducing a hopeless crush into our relationship."

"Your secret is safe with me," I assured her.

"Here, taste this." Ellie held up a spoonful of the soup for me to taste.

"Wow! I think this is it," I praised after I'd taken a sip. "What's different from the last batch?"

"Cream cheese," Ellie said. "I wrote everything down for you so you can make it for your grandpa for Christmas."

I took another sip. "This tastes exactly like the soup Grandma made. He's going to love it."

We carried our dinner to the small dining table that was tucked in a corner, near a widow overlooking the lake. It was a beautiful night. The snow that had blanketed the area had let up a bit, so that only flurries filled the air. The lights Zak and I had hung on the deck railing gave a festive feel to the exterior of my small home.

"I like this music," Ellie commented on the Christmas instrumental playing in the background. "It's Christmassy without being overpowering."

"It's actually an old CD I fished out of the Christmas decorations box. I forgot I even had it, to be honest, but after Zak and I finished the tree we decided to string lights around the cabinets in the kitchen, so I dug out my backup decorations. The CD was in a box I haven't used in a few years."

"The lights look nice," Ellie complimented. "It's so cozy and relaxing with the lights and the fire. You'll have to have Zak over when he gets back."

"If he ever gets back," I complained.

"I can't believe he still hasn't made it home," Ellie said sympathetically.

"Tell me about it. This whole thing has been bizarre. First he misses his flight due to an accident on the freeway, and then he can't find another flight until the next day, by which time a huge storm that has been blanketing the country decides to hit the East Coast, closing all the airports. I just hope he makes it back for the ball."

"He'll make it," Ellie reassured me.

"I hope so. I've really missed him."

Ellie smiled. "I've always known the two of you would end up together."

"How could you know? I've barely even been civil to him until a couple of months ago."

"Like you said, a best friend knows these things. Besides, your disdain for Zak has been so bizarre that the only explanation there could have been was repressed attraction. You guys are good together. I hope I can find someone who adores me as much as Zak obviously adores you."

"He is pretty great." I got up and began clearing the dishes. "I have cookies left from the exchange. Snowballs, chocolate peanut bars, and chocolate oat cookies."

"I'll take a chocolate oat cookie with coffee. Decaf, if you have it."

I started making the coffee while Ellie put the leftover food away. "Do you care if Charlie and Lambda finish off this salad?"

"No, that's fine. Charlie loves salad, although I've never tried giving it to Lambda."

"It looks like he enjoys it," Ellie said after she'd scraped the leftover veggies into the dogs' bowls. "Of course, Marlow and Spade are giving me the evil eye for not putting something yummy in their dishes."

"The cats don't like salad anyway. I have some leftover tuna in the refrigerator. I'll divide it between them."

Ellie took her coffee and cookie and sat down on the sofa in front of the fire while I dished out the cats' treat. "It seems like Hometown Christmas is going well in spite of the snow," Ellie commented.

"I talked to both Hazel and Willa today, and they're ecstatic," I shared. "There's just enough snow so that our visitors are getting a real feel for an old-fashioned mountain Christmas, but not enough to close the roads or cause delays. Having the event sandwiched between the community center and the park has worked out fantastically."

"You'd better be careful or they'll nominate you to do it again next year," Ellie teased.

Spade jumped up onto the sofa and curled up into Ellie's lap after he'd finished his treat. Ellie scratched him behind the ears and he began to purr. Marlow contented himself with the catnip mouse Ellie had brought with her, while Charlie and Lambda curled up on the rug in front of the fire. It was a perfect evening. Or at least it would have been if Zak had been there. I have to admit I was missing Levi as well. Christmas is a time for family, and not having *everyone* in attendance made me feel a little sad.

"Your phone is buzzing," Ellie informed me.

I glanced at my cell, which I had changed over to vibrate earlier in the day.

"Hello," I greeted.

I listened while Sheriff Salinger deflated the cloud of self-importance I'd been riding on since I'd once again solved a crime and caught the bad guy.

"But the bat?" I asked. I grimaced as Salinger replied. "Okay, thanks for the call."

"What's wrong?" Ellie asked.

"The blood on the bat I found in Drugger's bedroom didn't belong to Tanner."

"Oh God." Ellie cringed. "Who did it belong to?"

"It belonged to one of the guys on Drugger's baseball team, who was hit in the face by a wild pitch. Salinger didn't even realize the mistake until he finally caught up with Drugger and brought him in for questioning."

"I don't get why it took Salinger so long to realize that the blood on the bat didn't belong to Tanner. I mean, it's been days," Ellie pointed out.

"You know Salinger." I rolled my eyes. "He thought he'd tied up the case and basically moved on. He didn't even read the lab report until today. That guy is such a tool."

"So what now?" Ellie asked.

"I'm not sure," I admitted.

"I feel like we've explored all the possibilities in this case," Ellie said. "I suppose we could just leave it up to Salinger to figure out. It is, after all, his mess. I assume he isn't planning to reclose the community center?"

"No, it's too late for that. He agreed to leave it open. He's hoping I won't mention the mix-up to anyone until we can find the real killer."

"*We*?" Ellie asked.

"I guess he's pretty desperate."

"Okay, then, who, other than Drugger, would want to kill poor Earl? We're still operating on the assumption that Earl was the intended victim, right?"

I thought about it. I *was* certain that the intended victim was Earl after we'd exhausted the suspects who might want to kill Tanner, but now I wasn't so certain. Earl was the sweetest man in town. Everyone loved him. But Tanner? Tanner was a crotchety old guy who rubbed a lot of people the wrong way. The more I thought about it, the more I realized that he made the better victim. Now I just had to figure out who he'd aggravated enough to make them want to kill him.

******

"I'm sorry to call so late," Zak apologized from the other end of the line.

"No problem." I yawned and looked at the bedside clock. It was almost one a.m. and I was just preparing to get into bed. "I'm still up. Did your flight get in?"

"Finally. I'm in Bryton Lake. I figured you'd be asleep, but I've missed you and thought I'd call."

"Belinda?" I knew his assistant had gone to New York with him, and they'd ridden to the airport in the same car.

"She stayed on the East Coast to visit family."

I couldn't help but smile. "Why don't you stop by on your way home? I'll make you something to eat."

"Are you sure it's not too late? I could just come by tomorrow."

"I'm sure."

"Okay. I'll see you in thirty minutes."

After I hung up, I brushed my teeth and pulled on the sweats I'd been wearing that evening. I ran a brush through my hair, made the bed I had just turned down, and made my way downstairs. I tossed a log on the fire and plugged in the tree and lights. I lit a few candles and turned on the stereo. The serene and romantic atmosphere in the room in no way represented the fact that I'd had the most bizarre evening I'd had in quite some time. After Salinger's call, Ellie and I had gone over the list of suspects one final time, and all of a sudden it occurred to me exactly who the killer was. I'm not sure why I hadn't seen it before. I suppose I'd been distracted with the impending doom of the pet adoption and had my attention focused more on speed than anything else.

With the mood set, I wandered into the kitchen to put on a fresh pot of coffee and then began rummaging around for something to make Zak for dinner. Deciding that it was closer to breakfast than dinnertime, I quickly assembled a hash-brown casserole and put it in the oven. Then I set to mixing up a batch of cheesy bacon biscuits.

After I'd given it some thought, I'd realized that if Tanner were indeed the intended victim, then the killer had to be someone who knew about the change. The killer could have recognized Tanner when he or she waited for their little darling while they sat on Santa's knee, but my gut told me the killer most likely wasn't a parent. The only people who knew *for certain* that Tanner had replaced Earl were myself, Hazel, Ellie, and Penelope. Penelope never had liked Tanner, and it occurred to me that the idea that the man was trying to have her sister committed to a mental institution probably didn't sit well with her.

Especially since Agatha would most likely lose control of her half of the money from the sale of the house and boat if Tanner could convince a judge that she was incompetent. I'd called Salinger, who brought Penelope in for questioning. She didn't even put up a fight when Salinger accused her of the crime. She insisted that the man had gotten what he deserved for abandoning his wife after forty years of marriage.

By the time the casserole was heated, Zak was at the door.

"I missed you." Zak pulled me into his arms and kissed me in just the way I'd been fantasizing about for days.

"I missed you, too," I said and kissed him back.

"Something smells good." Zak took off his jacket and hung it on the coatrack by the door.

"Hash-brown casserole and cheesy bacon biscuits."

"Sounds perfect. I've been traveling back and forth around the country trying to get a flight home and haven't eaten anything but airline food for days."

"The airlines are that messed up?" I asked as I spooned the ham-and-cheese dish on a plate.

"They really are. The storm closed the airport for two days. When it finally reopened, there were people everywhere trying to get a flight out of the area. I had to go from New York to Miami and then catch a commuter flight to Atlanta. Just about the time I got there, the storm that had been lurking in the Gulf came ashore, and flights were delayed again. I rented a car and drove to St. Louis, where I was able to get a flight to Denver. It really was a madhouse."

"Are you home for a while?" I asked hopefully as Zak shoveled biscuits and casserole into his mouth.

"Until after the New Year for sure. After that, I may need to make another trip."

I refilled Zak's coffee and cleared his dishes. "I have cheesecake left if you want some."

"Sounds fantastic."

I went into the kitchen and sliced the cheesecake I'd made earlier in the week. I put it on one of my special Christmas dessert plates and poured Zak a glass of milk. When I returned to the living room, Zak was fast asleep on my little couch. He'd removed his snow-covered shoes when he'd come in, so I got a blanket from the chest and covered him. I turned off all the lights except the tree lights and tossed another log on the fire. Then I picked up Marlow and motioned for Charlie to follow me upstairs. Spade was curled up next to Zak and Lambda, who had missed his dad and was sound asleep on the rug next to the sofa.

As I got ready for bed for the second time, I sighed at the fact that, although Zak had slept at my boathouse a number of times if you counted the week after my accident in November, he'd yet to make it upstairs. Maybe Ellie wasn't too far off when she suggested new dresses for the ball. I think her exact word was something *shocking*.

Chapter 19

Christmas Eve

I woke to the sound of cursing, followed an instant later by the crash of glass shattering on the kitchen floor below my loft bedroom. The smell of coffee brewing and bacon frying filled the air as I opened my eyes and sat up. I looked around and tried to get my bearings, my brain struggling toward full wakefulness. I glanced at the rumpled sheets next to me and smiled. Since the *entire* bed was empty, I had to assume that Charlie and the cats had followed Zak downstairs.

I closed my eyes and laid back into the softness of my bed. I snuggled into my thick comforter as I remembered the magic of the previous evening. The thirty-six hours leading up to my perfect night had been a bit rocky, as I'd woken on Sunday morning to find Zak gone, leaving a note stating that he was going to be tied up the next couple of days but would pick me up at six o'clock for the Holly Ball as planned. I'd gone on a bit of a rant when Zak simply disappeared after having been gone for most of the month, but when he showed up for the ball in a horse-drawn sleigh holding a dozen red roses and a bottle of the finest champagne, my tantrum faded to enchantment.

Being a bit of a tomboy, I never really understood the infatuation little girls—and big girls, too, as I'm given to understand—have for the fairytale of Cinderella, but as Zak led me around the dance floor dressed in a perfectly tailored tuxedo, I understood for the first time how magical it could be to dress in a beautiful gown and dance the night away with your prince while he makes you feel like the most desirable woman in the world.

I slid out of bed and pulled on some thick sweatpants and a matching sweatshirt. As I slipped on my knee-high slippers, I glanced in the full-length mirror near the closet. It looked like the homely stepsister was back. The dress I'd bought during my shopping trip with Ellie on Sunday—dark-green velvet that fit me like a glove—had made me feel like a princess, but by the end of the evening I couldn't wait to take off the binding thing and slip into something a bit more comfortable.

Luckily for me, the zipper stuck, Zak offered to help, and the rest, as they say, was magic.

"Good morning, sleepyhead." Zak grinned as he handed me a cup of coffee.

"What time is it?" I yawned.

"Nine thirty."

"Nine thirty? I never sleep till nine thirty."

"We had a late night." Zak kissed my cheek.

I wrapped my arms around his neck and kissed him on the mouth. A long, lingering kiss that might have gone on for hours if Charlie hadn't gotten jealous and wedged himself between us. I reluctantly ended our kiss and bent down to pet the little traitor who had chosen to follow Zak downstairs rather than stay in bed with me.

"I hope you're hungry."

Zak returned to the kitchen and opened the oven as I greeted the cats in turn. "I made breakfast pie."

"Starving, but just a small piece. I'm meeting Ellie for lunch at one o'clock."

"I don't know," Zak cautioned. "Based on the way Rob and Ellie were melting into each other on the dance floor last night, she may have had a late night as well. Would you like a mimosa to go with your breakfast?"

"I'd love one."

Zak poured champagne and orange juice into a tall flute. I took my drink over to the sofa and sat down while Zak finished up in the kitchen. He had lit a fire and plugged in the tree and the rest of the lights I'd strung around my little boathouse. Soft music played on the stereo and, outside, gently falling snow drifted through the air. My home was warm and romantic, and I seriously considered calling Ellie and moving our lunch date until after Christmas.

Zak set plates of cheesy breakfast pie and homemade biscuits on the coffee table in front of us. He refilled our coffee cups before joining me on the sofa.

"I have something for you." Zak handed me a box.

"But it's not Christmas yet."

"I know. I want you to have it now. Open it."

Inside the long green box was a necklace with a delicate chain and a *Z* in the center. In the middle of the *Z* was a beautiful diamond that I was sure was big enough to be seen from across the room. "Wow. It's beautiful." I slowly lifted it from the box. "*Z* for Zoe?"

"Or Zak." Zak smiled as I lifted my hair and he clasped it around my neck. "Unless having your guy's initial on your chest is too corny; then it can stand for Zoe."

"I like corny," I assured him, "but I don't have anything to give you." I never had decided on a gift for him.

Zak smiled. "Yes you do."

We never did eat those eggs.

Grandma Donovan's Cheesy Potato Soup

12 cups potatoes, peeled and diced
1 bunch of leeks or green onions, washed and chopped
8 cups chicken broth
4 chicken bouillon cubes

Boil until potatoes are tender. Mash potatoes into small chunks in broth. Do not drain.

Lower heat and add:

1 cube butter
1 8 oz. package of cream cheese
2 cups of heavy whipping cream

When cream cheese is completely dissolved add:

8 cups shredded cheddar cheese
2 cups of grated Parmesan cheese
Salt and pepper to taste

Simmer until cheese is melted and soup thickens.

Notes:

Add cheese slowly, stirring constantly until blended.

You can add broccoli, cauliflower, or both for variety.

This soup makes a *lot* but is good as a leftover. In fact, many times Grandma made the soup the day before, refrigerated it, and then reheated.

Author Bio

USA Today best-selling author Kathi Daley lives in beautiful Lake Tahoe with her husband Ken. When she isn't writing, she likes spending time hiking the miles of desolate trails surrounding her home. She has authored more than a hundred books in twelve series. Find out more about her books at www.kathidaley.com